FRED BOWEN series
SPORTS STORY

FRED BOWEN

PEACHTREE
ATLANTA

Published by
PEACHTREE PUBLISHERS
1700 Chattahoochee Avenue
Atlanta, Georgia 30318-2112
www.peachtree-online.com

Text © 2013 by Fred Bowen

Cover design by Thomas Gonzalez and Maureen Withee
Book design by Melanie McMahon Ives
Printed in December 2012 by R. R. Donnelley and Sons, Harrisonburg, Virginia
10 9 8 7 6 5 4 3 2 1 (hardcover)
10 9 8 7 6 5 4 3 2 1 (trade paperback)
First edition

Library of Congress Cataloging-in-Publication Data
    Bowen, Fred.
        Perfect game / written by Fred Bowen.
            p. cm.
        Summary: Isaac is a perfectionist, especially when it comes to baseball, and is unable to cope when things go wrong until his coach asks him to help out with a Unified Sports basketball team on which intellectually disabled and other kids play together.
        ISBN 13: 978-1-56145-701-4 / ISBN 10: 1-56145-701-9 (hardcover)
        ISBN 13: 978-1-56145-625-3 / ISBN 10: 1-56145-625-X (trade paper-back)
        [1. Perfectionism (Personality trait)--Fiction. 2. Basketball--Fiction. 3. People with mental disabilities--Fiction. 4. Baseball--Fiction. 5. Self-control--Fiction.] I. Title.
        PZ7.B6724Per 2013
        [Fic]--dc23
                                                                2012027792

For Joanne Pasternack,
who many years ago got me
thinking about this story.

One hour to game time! Isaac Burnett thought as he ran upstairs to his bedroom. *And I'm pitching!*

He headed straight to his dresser and opened the top drawer. The rest of his room was a mess, but his baseball uniform—shirt, pants, and socks—lay neatly in the drawer, just the way he kept it between games.

Isaac began putting on his uniform the same way he did for every Giants game. First he pulled his baseball socks up to his knees, making sure the stripes along each side were straight. Next he pulled his white baseball pants over his socks and tugged at each pant leg so that it ended exactly halfway between his knee and his ankle.

Isaac then unfolded the special blue undershirt (the same blue as the letters that spelled out "Giants" on his game shirt) and pulled it over his head. He slipped his arms into his game shirt and buttoned it slowly, taking care to leave the top button unbuttoned. He didn't want it scratching his neck when he uncorked his best fastball.

He raced to his parents' bedroom and stood shoeless before the full-length mirror that hung on their closet door. He checked his uniform from every angle. He adjusted his right pant leg just a bit so that it was perfectly even with the left.

Now he was ready for his hat, which was right where he'd left it—on top of his dresser with the bill of the cap wrapped around a baseball and held snug with two rubber bands. He slipped off the bands, then put the baseball back onto the dresser.

Sweeping his hair back, Isaac placed the hat slowly and carefully on his head. Then he slid his right thumb and forefinger across the bill of the cap. It curved in a smooth, gentle arc, just the way he liked it.

All of his other hats were battered and jumbled together in a basket downstairs, but he saved his Giants hat for game days.

All he needed now were his cleats. They sat cleaned and ready, along with Isaac's baseball glove, at the back door. His mother and father didn't allow cleats in the house.

Before he headed downstairs, he returned to his parents' bedroom and checked the mirror one last time. Everything was just the way he liked it.

The socks.

The pants.

The shirt.

And last but not least, the hat.

Isaac was ready to pitch. He stared unsmiling at himself in the mirror. "Eighteen outs," he said in a determined voice. "That's what I'm going to get today. No runs, no hits, no errors, no walks. Eighteen straight outs. A perfect game."

Isaac turned toward the Giants catcher Alex Oquendo, crouched behind home plate. He saw Alex flash the one-finger signal and slide his glove slightly to his right. Fastball to the outside corner.

Isaac nodded and started his windup. He rocked back with his knee up high and then whipped the ball and his body forward with all his might. The ball flashed out of his hand and smacked into the catcher's glove. Alex never moved a muscle.

"Strike three!" The umpire raised his right hand into a fist. "You're out."

A perfect pitch! Isaac punched the pocket of his glove and walked off the pitcher's mound to the cheers of the crowd. It was the bottom of the fourth, and Isaac had a perfect game going. No runs, no hits, no errors, no walks.

Isaac's father, Alan Burnett, was in the stands, cheering the loudest. "All right, Isaac!" he shouted through cupped hands. "Six more outs, buddy. Six more outs."

Mr. Park, the Giants coach, was shouting too. "All right, good inning! No runs, no hits, no errors." He glanced at the lineup posted on the dugout wall. "Let's get some more runs this inning. Max, Caden, and Ben are up. Everybody hits."

Isaac headed to the far end of the bench.

His teammates left him alone. They knew that some major league players considered it bad luck to talk to a pitcher when he had a no-hitter going.

He checked the scoreboard.

INNING	1	2	3	4	5	6
Royals	0	0	0	0		
Giants	0	1	1			

The Giants led the Royals 2–0. Isaac glanced over his shoulder to his father and mother in the stands. His dad gave him a quick thumbs-up.

Isaac stretched out his legs and thought back over the first four innings. Twelve Royals batters. Twelve outs. He was on a roll. This could be the day he pitched his perfect game.

Jackson Rhodes—the Giants third baseman—sat down on the bench. "You're throwing great," Jackson whispered, sliding a little closer. Isaac didn't mind him coming over. Jackson had been his best friend since kindergarten.

"Yeah," Isaac agreed. "I feel good. I got my best stuff today. Everything's working."

"Keep it up," Jackson said. "We'll get you some more runs."

"Don't sweat it," Isaac said. "We've got enough runs already."

Crack! Max Crosby, the Giants left fielder, smacked a liner into the gap and took off. He rounded first base and sprinted toward second, slipping his foot under the tag. Safe!

Isaac smiled and nodded while Jackson and the rest of the team jumped to their feet and cheered wildly.

"All right, Max!"

"That's the way to get things started!"

"Let's get some more hits!"

Jackson sat back down next to Isaac but kept his eyes on the game. "Come on, Caden. Be a hitter!"

Standing in the third-base coach's box, Coach Park touched the bill of his cap, swept his right hand down his left arm, and clapped his hands.

Isaac elbowed Jackson. "Coach wants Caden to bunt," he whispered.

His friend nodded. "With the way you're pitching, I guess he figures if we score one more run we're a cinch to win."

Max was ready to run. He had one foot on second base and the other stretched toward third. As the pitch came in, Caden squared around in the batter's box and held the bat level in front of him. The ball plunked against his bat and rolled slowly out toward third. Max took off. The Royals third baseman rushed in, grabbed the ball

7

bare-handed, and threw to first for the easy out.

The Giants had a runner on third with one out. Ben Badillo, the Giants shortstop, stepped up to bat.

"Come on, Ben!" Jackson yelled from the bench. "Drive him home." Ben smacked a high hopper over the pitcher's mound and through the infield. Max raced toward home and crossed the plate with his hands held high. The Giants were ahead, 3–0!

A fly out and a strikeout later, the Giants ran out to the field and Isaac walked to the mound for the top of the fifth. Two innings to go. Six outs to get.

"We're up by three runs," Coach Park called out to his players as they took their positions on the field. "Just throw strikes, Isaac. No walks. Make them be hitters."

You mean make them be NO hitters, Isaac thought as he toed the pitching rubber. *Six more outs. No way the Royals are going to wreck my perfect game.*

Isaac started the inning fast, blazing three straight fastballs by the Royals cleanup hitter. One out, five more to go.

The Giants infielders cheered him on.

"Way to go, Isaac!"

"No batter, no batter!"

"One-two-three inning!"

The next Royals batter knocked a sharp grounder to Isaac's right. Isaac panicked but Jackson was ready. He gobbled up the grounder, steadied himself, and fired the ball to first base, nipping the runner by a step.

Out!

Isaac let out a deep breath and pointed to Jackson. "Great play."

Jackson smiled and held up two fingers. "Two outs," he called to the Giants outfielders.

Isaac stared in at the hitter stepping into the batter's box. *Okay, get this guy*, Isaac told himself. *Then it's the bottom of the order and a perfect game. No sweat.*

On the third pitch, the Royals batter sent a slow bouncer spinning toward third base. Jackson charged hard, but the ball took a funny hop and bounced off the heel of his glove. Just like that, the runner was safe at first and Isaac's perfect game was gone.

"My error," Jackson said, tapping his chest and tossing the ball to Isaac. "You still got your no-hitter."

Coach Park clapped his hands and shouted, "Shake it off, Jackson! Tough hop. Remember, we have a force play at second base. Get the easy out."

Isaac tried to concentrate, but he kept thinking about the bad-hop error. He was pitching great. He had a perfect game going and Jackson blew it.

Four pitches later, another Royals batter was on base with a walk. Isaac paced around the mound to calm himself down.

"Come on, Isaac!" his father shouted. "Throw strikes!"

Isaac got back into position and took a deep breath. He toed the pitching rubber and fired. But the moment the ball left his hand, he knew he was in trouble again. A belt-high fastball across the heart of the plate. An easy pitch to hit.

Crack!

Isaac froze as he watched the line drive go deep into center field and the Royals runner on second speeding toward home. Jared Jankowski fielded the ball cleanly, but his throw skipped by the catcher and smacked against the backstop.

"Come on, Isaac!" Coach Park shouted, pointing behind home plate where Isaac should have been. "Back Alex up. Get your head in the game!"

But Isaac couldn't get back into his pitching groove. After his next two pitches sailed wide, the Giants infielders traded worried glances. But they kept the patter going, trying to pump him up.

"Come on, Isaac, one more out!"

"No batter. No batter."

"Bear down! Nothing but strikes."

Isaac reared back and threw the next fastball with all his strength.

Crack!

Isaac turned quickly. He saw Jared racing back for the ball rocketing to left center field. It almost got away, but Jared leaped high and snagged it for the final out of the inning. Isaac blew out the big breath he had been holding in.

Coach Park pulled Isaac aside as he entered the dugout. "I'm going to have Liam pinch-hit for you and bring in Charlie to pitch the last inning."

Isaac nodded silently. He didn't want to pitch anyway, now that his perfect game was gone.

"Good job," Coach said as he patted Isaac on the shoulder. "You just let things get away from you a little bit in the last inning. But you gave us a chance to win. That's what a good starting pitcher is supposed to do."

Isaac put on his jacket and slumped down on the end of the bench. The spring afternoon felt colder now that he was out of the game.

Jackson came over and stood in front of Isaac. "Sorry about the error," he said. "I should've had it. The ball took a weird hop."

"Yeah," Isaac said, barely looking up. "You should've had it."

"Hey, lighten up. We'll get you the win,"

Jackson said, turning away. "In case you haven't noticed, we're still ahead."

Isaac sat still and silent. He hardly noticed his teammates cheering and banging their hands against the dugout screen, or the four-run rally that put the Giants safely ahead, 7–1.

Isaac wasn't thinking about the Giants hits, runs, or even their win. He was thinking about the one bad-hop error and the perfect game that had slipped away.

Clear the table, please," Isaac's mother said. "I've got to make a quick phone call."

"No worries," Isaac said. He began collecting the dishes from the small dining room table.

Isaac's father looked outside. The rays of the early evening sun slanted past the houses in the neighborhood. "We've still got a little sunlight left," he said. "You want to practice your throwing?"

"Sure," Isaac said as he started out of the room.

"Whoa, not so fast. You have to finish clearing the table first." Mr. Burnett grabbed the three water glasses and carried them to the sink. "Come on, I'll help."

Isaac and his dad talked baseball as they loaded the dishwasher.

"So when's your next game?"

"Saturday."

"Who are you playing?"

"The Yankees."

"You going to pitch?"

Isaac shook his head. "I already pitched five innings this week, so Coach Park's going to start Charlie Anderson. But I might pitch an inning in relief."

"Wow, you guys are fast workers," said Isaac's mom as she came back into the kitchen. "Talking baseball again?" She grabbed a glass and got some water from the refrigerator.

"Yeah," said Isaac. "I was telling Dad about our next game."

"What's your record?" she asked.

"I'm 3–0," Isaac answered, thinking of his three pitching wins.

"I meant the team's record."

"Oh." Isaac paused and thought for a moment. "I think it's 5–2. Let me check."

The Giants schedule was stuck to the refrigerator door with a round magnet shaped like a baseball. Isaac had marked the score on the schedule after each game.

GIANTS SEASON SCHEDULE
All Games Played at Upton Memorial Field
Coach Michael Park

Date	Opponent	Time
Sat. April 21	Yankees W 2-1	2 p.m.
Wed. April 25	Royals W 9-7	5:30 p.m.
Fri. April 27	Orioles W 11-2	5:30 p.m.
Thur. May 3	Rangers L 9-4	5:30 p.m.
Sat. May 5	Pirates L 4-2	noon
Tues. May 8	Nationals W 5-0	5:30 p.m.
Sat. May 12	Rockies L 5-3	10 a.m.
Thur. May 17	Royals W 7-1	5:30 p.m.
Sat. May 19	Yankees	4 p.m.
Wed. May 23	Orioles	5:30 p.m.
Sat. May 26	Rangers	2 p.m.
Wed. May 30	Nationals	5:30 p.m.
Fri. June 1	Pirates	5:30 p.m.
Thur. June 7	Yankees	5:30 p.m.
Sat. June 9	Rockies	noon

"No, we're 5–3."

"If you keep pitching the way you have been," Mr. Burnett said with a smile, "you'll be a shoo-in for the Thunderbolts."

"Who are the Thunderbolts?" his mom asked.

"They're the league's summer all-star team and—," his dad began.

Isaac interrupted, barely able to contain his excitement. "The T-bolts have all the best kids from the Junior League, Mom! They play in tournaments during the summer. It would be so cool to make the team."

"It does sound cool."

"And he's got a good chance of making it," Isaac's dad said. "But right now we need to hurry up and get outside. We don't have much time to throw."

Isaac and his dad grabbed their gloves from the corner basket and hurried out, letting the screen door slap shut behind them. Without a word, they jogged out to their familiar spots: two worn patches of dirt 52 feet apart—the standard pitching distance for Junior League games. Mr. Burnett used his foot to sweep away some dirt from the hard rubber home plate he had placed there years ago. On the other bare patch, Isaac windmilled his right arm to loosen up his shoulder.

"Let's warm up with a quick game of catch," Isaac's dad suggested.

"Okay."

The baseball flew back and forth between Isaac and his father. The only sounds were the *whoosh* of the ball through the air and the *smack* of it hitting the leather gloves. Mr. Burnett finally interrupted the steady *whoosh-smack* rhythm and said, "Okay, let's throw some real pitches now."

"Sure!" Isaac said. He always wanted to pitch.

His dad crouched behind home plate. Isaac went into his windup, lifted his knee, and drove hard toward the plate. The ball thwacked dead center in his father's mitt.

Isaac threw a steady stream of fastballs, and his father sent back a steady stream of suggestions.

"Don't lift your leg up too high, you'll lose

your balance. Remember: push off the rubber every time. Your power comes from your legs, not just your arm. Keep your eye on the target."

Isaac's dad looked up at the fading light. "Do you want to pitch to a few batters before we have to go in?"

"Sure," Isaac answered. "You want to do signals?"

"Yeah, one finger for a fastball and I'll wiggle all four for a changeup." Isaac's dad stood up, punched a quick fist into his catcher's mitt, and repositioned himself behind the plate. "All right, first batter. Let's say he's a righty." He flashed one finger and set up on the inside part of the plate.

Isaac sizzled a fastball right into his father's glove.

"Strike one!"

Mr. Burnett shifted slightly, and this time he set up on the outside corner of the plate. He flashed one finger.

Isaac nodded. Keeping his eyes on the target, he let go another blazing fastball.

"Strike two!" his dad called, smiling. "No balls, two strikes. How about a changeup? Keep it low and away. Maybe he'll swing at it."

Isaac moved the ball back in his grip and slid a third finger across the seams. After all his practicing, he had an awesome changeup. He threw it just as hard as his fastball, but it sailed slow and fell away at the end. Batters would swing too soon and miss the ball by a mile.

"Good pitch!" His father was beaming. "A lot of kids will swing at a changeup when you have two strikes on them." He threw the ball back to Isaac. "But let's say the batter held back and didn't swing. The count's one ball, two strikes." He flashed one finger. "Fastball. Let's finish him with this pitch."

Isaac's fastball rocketed toward the plate's outside edge. Isaac's father shifted his glove slightly and snapped the ball out of the air.

"Ball two!" he shouted.

"What?" Isaac exploded. "That was right on the outside corner!"

"I had to move my glove," his father replied with a shake of his head.

Isaac stomped his foot on the dirt. "You only moved it a couple of inches," he argued. "It was still a strike!"

"You know the game," Isaac's dad said as he tossed the ball back. "If I have to move my glove—even an inch—it's a ball. It's got to be perfect to be a strike." Then he added, "Remember—practice doesn't make perfect. *Perfect* practice makes perfect. And who knows, maybe enough perfect practice will get you a perfect game."

Isaac knew the drill all right. He and his father had played it countless times on evenings like this. Batter after batter, pitch after pitch as the sun set and the lights from the porch spilled out onto the backyard.

Same home plate.

Same pitching rubber.

Same 52 feet.

Same rules. If his father had to move his glove—even an inch—it was a ball.

And his dad always said the same thing:

Practice doesn't make perfect. Perfect *practice makes perfect.*

His father set up on the outside edge of the plate again. "Remember," he said to Isaac. "Two balls, two strikes. You want to make it happen on this pitch."

Isaac stared hard at his dad, pressed his lips tight, and hurled a fastball that flew like a laser to his father's glove.

This time, his father didn't have to move a muscle.

"Strike three!" he shouted. "Perfect."

Chapter 4

H ey Isaac!" Coach Park shouted down the bench. "You're pitching next inning. Start warming up."

Isaac tapped Alex Oquendo on the knee. "Come on, Alex, warm me up."

Alex shook his head. "I can't. I'm up third this inning."

"Who made the last out?" Coach Park asked.

"I did," Jackson said.

Coach Park pointed to the bullpen. "Go with Isaac and warm him up. Be sure to take a catcher's mask."

Isaac and Jackson grabbed their gloves and jogged out to the bullpen. They glanced at the scoreboard.

INNING	1	2	3	4	5	6
Giants	0	3	2	0	0	
Yankees	1	0	0	1	2	

After five innings the Giants were clinging to a one-run lead, 5–4.

Jackson elbowed Isaac. "Coach is bringing you in for the big save," he teased. "I hope you like pressure." Jackson cupped his hands around his mouth and made his voice sound like a ballpark announcer's. "And now pitching for the Giants. Number 26. I-saaaac. Burrrrr-nnnnet."

"No worries," Isaac said without a trace of a smile. "I'll be fine."

Jackson crouched behind the bullpen's home plate. "How long will it take you to warm up?"

"About a dozen pitches," Isaac said.

"You'd better hurry, there's already one out."

Two more Giants outs and fifteen warm-up pitches later, Isaac was heading to the pitcher's mound. The score was still 5–4. Coach Park chattered nervously as he collected the bats around the dugout. "Come on, Isaac, nothing but strikes. Infielders, ready positions. Nothing gets by you. Knock everything down."

Alex got into his crouch and pulled down his mask. "Come on, Isaac!" he shouted. "Really bring it!"

Isaac took a deep breath and fired a fastball past the Yankees leadoff hitter.

Strike one.

The Giants infield cheered.

"All right, Isaac. Blow it right by 'em!"

"No hitter, no hitter."

"You're the man, Isaac."

Alex signaled for another fastball and edged over to the outside corner. Isaac reached back for a little extra on his fastball. It flew so fast the batter barely saw it.

Strike two.

Alex signaled for another fastball. Isaac shook his head. He was thinking back to his backyard practice sessions and could almost hear his father's voice. *A lot of kids will swing at a changeup when you have two strikes on them.* Alex wiggled his fingers for a changeup. Isaac nodded.

Just like in his backyard, Isaac's pitch took a surprise dip as it sailed in. The Yankee tried to check his swing, but it was too late.

"Strike three!" yelled the umpire. "You're out!"

"Make it a one-two-three inning, Isaac!" Jackson shouted from third base. "One-two-three inning!"

The next batter fouled off the first two pitches. No balls, two strikes. Isaac was ahead of him. This time Alex wiggled his fingers, calling for the changeup. Isaac let a little smile show at the corner of his mouth and nodded. He went into his windup and threw hard. The ball stayed low and away. The batter swung and missed.

Strike three!

The Giants infielders shouted even louder as they paced around the infield dirt.

"That's two down!"

"One more, Isaac! One more."

"Nothing but strikes! One-two-three. One-two-three."

Isaac recognized the next Yankees batter, Noah Jamison. *He played for the Thunderbolts last summer,* Isaac thought. *Better be careful with him.*

"Go right after him!" Coach Park called out, clapping his hands. "No free passes."

He'll be looking at the first pitch, hoping to get a walk, Isaac thought as he nodded at the fastball sign. He blazed a fastball right down the middle.

Strike one.

Then Isaac came back with a diving changeup that completely fooled Noah.

Strike two.

The Giants and their fans were on their feet cheering. Isaac could hear his father's voice above the others. "One more, Isaac, one more! No batter, no batter!"

Isaac tried to block out the noise and concentrate. He was one throw away from a perfect inning: nine strikes on nine pitches. There was no way he was going to let Noah get his bat on the ball.

Alex set his catcher's mitt on the razor edge of the outside corner. Isaac went into his windup and then let go, squeezing every ounce of his strength into the pitch. The ball streaked by Noah in a blur. He never took his bat off his shoulder.

"Ball one," the umpire called out.

"Ball?" Isaac shouted in disbelief. "That was a strike!"

The umpire pulled off his mask, shot a glance at Coach Park, and pointed to the mound.

Coach Park hustled out and put his arm around Isaac's shoulder. "Take it easy, take it easy. Remember, the umpire can throw you out of the game for arguing. That means you'd miss the next game too. We don't want that."

Isaac was still steaming. "That was a strike," he insisted, almost spitting out the words. "Alex never moved his glove. It was perfect. Right on the outside corner."

"Okay, okay, settle down," Coach Park said softly.

"I was pitching a perfect inning and he ruined it."

"We don't need a perfect inning, Isaac. We just need a win. One more strike. You're doing great." He patted Isaac on the shoulder. "One more out. Let's get the win for your team." Coach gave him a few moments to calm down, then walked back to the dugout.

Isaac took a deep breath and zeroed in on Alex, waiting for his sign. He kept shaking his head until Alex signaled for a fastball on the outside corner. The same pitch as last time.

Isaac once again poured everything he had into the fastball. This time, Noah swung hard. And missed.

Strike three!

The Giants had won, 5–4.

Isaac's teammates swarmed him, but he didn't feel like a hero. He was still thinking about the umpire's call.

His father came down from the bleachers with a smile a mile wide. "Three straight strikeouts," he crowed. "Talk about a perfect inning!"

"Dad, it wasn't perfect."

"Well, *almost* perfect. Nine out of ten pitches were strikes. You can't do much better than that."

"Great game. You did a terrific job!" his mother said. "We'll see you at home. You're going to ride your skateboard, right?"

"Yeah." Isaac loved riding his skateboard after a game. He liked having that time by himself. And he definitely wanted to be by himself now.

"Okay," his mom said. "We'll take your equipment bag. Be careful."

"See you at home, champ," his father said, grabbing Isaac's bag.

Coach Park wandered over as the Burnetts left. "Good job, Isaac," he said. "Although I thought you were going to lose it when the umpire made that call."

"It should've been a strike!" Isaac couldn't stop thinking about it. "That pitch was absolutely perfect."

"Isaac, remember what I told you out there on the mound? You need to—"

"But Coach, I was so close to a perfect inning."

Coach Park didn't respond right away. He looked as if he was thinking of something, weighing it in his mind.

"Do you play basketball?" he finally asked Isaac.

"Yeah, I play on a recreational team in the winter," Isaac said, wondering why Coach Park was asking him about that. "I'm not that great, though. I'm a lot better at baseball."

"I was just thinking...would you like to help me with another team...a basketball team that I coach?"

Isaac felt trapped. He didn't want to do it. But he didn't want to say no either. After all, Coach Park could put in a good word for him with the Thunderbolts coach.

"Like I said, I'm not that great at basketball. I don't know what I can teach them."

"That's okay. Who knows, maybe *you'll* learn something."

Isaac wondered what his coach meant by that. "I don't know. When do you guys play?"

"We practice at two o'clock every Sunday afternoon at Landmark School. My daughter Maya and a bunch of other kids will be there."

"Um, okay. I guess I can try it."

Just then the phone on Coach Park's belt rang out the notes to "Take Me Out to the Ball Game." He answered the call as he swung the equipment bag into the back of his beat-up pickup truck, then listened for a moment. "Yeah, okay. I'm leaving right now. I'll be there in ten minutes."

Coach Park looked back at Isaac. "I'll see you Sunday, a little before two, okay?" He climbed into the driver's seat.

"Sunday at two," Isaac agreed. He walked away from the truck, then thought of something and turned back.

"Hey, Coach!" Isaac called. "What kind of team is it?"

The rattle of the old truck's engine drowned out his words. He watched as Coach Park revved the motor and took off, the truck wheels spitting back dirt.

I guess I'll find out on Sunday, Isaac thought.

saac heard a distant church bell ringing out the time as he ran to Landmark School.

Bong...bong.

Two o'clock, Isaac thought. *I'm late.*

He spotted some kids throwing a mini football around the school parking lot. "Where's the gym?" he asked. The kids pointed to an open door at the side of the school.

Isaac rushed down a half dozen steps into the school and followed the sound of basketballs pounding against the floor. He almost knocked into a boy about his age dressed in a yellow jersey. The kid just stood in the doorway watching the action.

The scene inside the gym was chaos—nothing at all like Coach Park's baseball practices. Some players were taking shots at different baskets, others were dribbling in unpredictable patterns. Two kids kept bounce-passing a ball back and forth. About half of the players wore identical bright yellow T-shirts like the kid's in the doorway. The others wore white shirts.

Coach Park waved at Isaac. "Over here!" he called. "It's good to see you." He turned to a girl in a white shirt chasing a ball under the bleachers. "Maya, why don't you show Isaac what to do."

A girl who looked a little older than Isaac—about fifteen—jogged over with the basketball. She wore gray sweatpants and her dark hair was pulled back in a ponytail. "Hi, I'm Maya," she said, smiling. "Coach Park is my dad. He said you'd be coming today."

A big kid in a Washington Nationals baseball cap and one of the yellow shirts walked up to Isaac and stuck out his hand. "Hi, I'm Theo," he said. "Who are you?"

Isaac was a bit confused, but shook Theo's hand. "I'm Isaac. I...um..."

Maya pushed Theo gently away. "Come on, Theo," she said. "You're supposed to be warming up, remember?"

Theo looked at Maya. "That's a pretty T-shirt," he said. "I like that T-shirt."

"Yeah, I know," Maya said, still pushing. "Go get a ball and warm up now. I'm showing Isaac around."

Theo walked away but he didn't look for a ball. He headed toward the bleachers and shook hands with a parent sitting in the front row. Isaac could hear Theo introducing himself again. "Hi, I'm Theo."

"What's with him?" Isaac asked.

Maya laughed. "Oh, Theo?" she said. "He's a real politician. He likes to meet and greet everybody."

"He doesn't look like much of a basketball player." Isaac watched the boy shaking hands with other parents in the stands. "Even if he is a big guy. And what's with the hat at basketball practice?"

"He's a big Nats fan."

"He doesn't wear it during games, does he?"

Maya eyed Isaac. "Did my dad tell you anything about our team?"

Isaac looked around the gym. The kids didn't look like any basketball team he'd ever played on. There was even a girl in a wheelchair and a teenager on a pair of metal crutches, the kind with arm cuffs and handgrips.

"Not really," Isaac answered. "He just asked me if I played basketball and whether I wanted to help with a team he coached."

"So he never told you this is a Unified Sports team?" Maya asked.

"Unified Sports? What's that?"

"It's a Special Olympics thing," she said. "See the kids in the yellow shirts? They have ID, intellectual disabilities—"

"You mean they're retarded?" Isaac blurted out.

Maya glanced at a group of parents sitting on the bleachers. "That's not a word we use," she said softly. "And you shouldn't either. It's really not nice."

"Yeah, but that's what they are," Isaac insisted. "I mean, they can't really play. Not in a real game."

"They're better than you think," Maya said. "And the team includes partners. The kids like us in the white shirts—"

"Like those two kids helping the boy on crutches with that weird green ball?"

"It's a lightweight ball. But, yeah. Avi and Bella are Unified Sports partners like me. Our job is to rebound and pass and get the ball to the Special Olympics players— we call them the athletes—so they can score. They're spotting Danny right now. He's a little wobbly without his crutches."

"A kid with crutches is allowed to play?"

"My dad lets him play, and Shontelle too. She's the girl in the wheelchair. They both have intellectual disabilities like the other kids. In a competitive Unified Sports program, I don't think you can have crutches and wheelchairs on the court. It's a safety thing. But we're more like a rec team and my dad's pretty careful."

"Yeah, but—" Before Isaac could finish, Coach Park blew his whistle. The partners and the athletes began to gather around him.

"Stick with me," Maya whispered to Isaac. "I'll show you the ropes. Just remember to try to get the ball to the players in the yellow jerseys."

Coach Park looked beyond the circle of players to the kid in the doorway. "Hey, Kevin, you want to join us?"

The boy turned his face toward the wall.

"Okay," Coach Park said cheerfully. "No problem."

"What's with that kid Kevin?" Isaac asked Maya in a low voice. "I mean, he's dressed like he's gonna play."

"He's really shy. I've never seen him play. He just watches."

"The whole practice?"

"Yup. The whole practice."

"That's weird," Isaac said.

Maya shrugged. "That's Kevin."

Coach Park started the practice and let Phoenix, a Special Olympics player, lead everyone in warm-up exercises. Phoenix barked out orders like an army drill sergeant while the players stretched.

"Okay now, time for the Start and Stop Whistle Drill!" Coach Park shouted after a few minutes. "You guys know what to do!"

The players quickly lined up against the gym wall.

Fweeet! Coach Park let out a sharp blast with his whistle and everyone started running forward. The kid with the crutches worked hard to keep up. Shontelle, the girl in the wheelchair, leaned forward, rocking back and forth, as Maya jogged behind her, pushing her chair. The faster Maya pushed, the faster Shontelle rocked.

Coach Park blew his whistle a second time and everyone skidded to a stop. He blew it again, and they took off again. They knew the drill well and seemed to love all the stopping and starting.

"Good work! Remember to play the whistle," Coach Park called after a final trip up the floor. "Okay, let's scrimmage. I want Maya and Shontelle, Isaac, Theo, Phoenix, and Lucas on one team."

"We got six players," Isaac said as the coach called out the names for the other team.

"I have to push Shontelle's chair," Maya explained. "And anyway the other team has seven kids."

"Thirteen kids on the court? I don't get it."

Lucas, a player with a short square body, hugged Maya and Shontelle.

"You will," Maya said, returning Lucas's hug. "Just get the ball to Theo, Lucas, and Phoenix so they can score."

The other team dribbled the ball down-court.

"Hands up on defense!" Maya shouted. Everyone, including Shontelle, shot their hands into the air.

A player on the other team stopped his dribble, then started up again.

"Hey, he's traveling!" Isaac yelled. "That's a double dribble."

"Keep playing," Coach Park ordered.

Isaac grabbed the rebound and started to dribble upcourt. "Pass off!" Coach shouted. "Pass it to Phoenix."

Isaac bounced a pass to Phoenix, who took a few quick dribbles, then tucked the ball under his arm and weaved his way toward the basket. Finally Phoenix found a spot he liked and pushed up a left-handed shot.

Swish!

The whole gym erupted. Everyone was cheering—Phoenix's teammates, the kids on the bench, the parents in the stands, even the kids on the other team. Phoenix loved the attention and spun happily around. He twirled his finger as if painting a picture in the air. Then he stopped and pumped both fists. "Yes!" he shouted.

The game continued until Coach Park blew his whistle. "Let's give Shontelle a shot now," he called. "Avi and Bella, grab the barrel."

The two partners snapped into action. They grabbed a big gray barrel with a sign plastered across it: Special Olympics. Not for Trash! They dragged it under the basket and held it up at about shoulder height. Maya wheeled Shontelle, who had the basketball in her lap, over near the barrel. The players on the court stood back, giving her plenty of room.

Shontelle sat up straight in her chair and lifted the ball with both hands, struggling to keep control. She pushed the ball up the side of the barrel with everyone rooting for her.

"Come on, Shontelle!"

"You can do it!"

"Keep pushing."

Shontelle kept working at it until the ball teetered on the edge and fell in. Everyone in the gym went wild. "All right!" Coach Park yelled above the others. Lucas gave a smiling Shontelle another hug.

"Great basket!" Maya shouted.

Basket? That's not a real basket, Isaac thought. *Even in this kind of game.*

Coach Park changed up the teams and Isaac walked to the sidelines. He grabbed a basketball and started flipping up short shots to the basket closest to the door. Kevin was still standing in the doorway watching.

"You want a shot?" Isaac asked, faking a quick pass to him. Kevin's hands reached out, almost like a reflex.

"Go ahead." Isaac snapped him a bounce pass.

Kevin bobbled the ball, but then pulled it tight. He looked to the basket, took a few quick dribbles away from the doorway, and then sent up a funny-looking two-handed jumper.

Swish!

Surprised, Isaac grabbed the rebound and bounced him another pass. "Hey, nice shot. Try it again."

Another shot. *Swish!*

Isaac grabbed the ball. Another pass. Another shot. This time the ball rolled around the rim a couple of times, then dropped in.

Coach Park blew his whistle. "Okay, guys. Let's circle up!"

Kevin stepped back and took his usual spot in the doorway.

Isaac joined the circle next to Maya. "That kid's got a loosey-goosey shot," he whispered, "but they keep going in."

"What are you talking about?" Maya asked. "Do you mean Kevin?"

"Yeah. The kid who always stands in the doorway. He hit three in a row."

"When?"

"Just now. It only took him about fifteen seconds."

"You're kidding."

"I'm serious. Two of them were nothing but net."

Maya was suddenly excited. "I've got to tell my dad. Kevin's never done that."

"You mean hit three in a row? It's not *that* big a deal."

Maya shook her head. "I don't think he's ever taken a shot, period. It's a *huge* deal." Maya looked straight at Isaac. "You've got to come back next week. To work with Kevin."

Isaac hesitated. He still had his doubts about this Unified Sports stuff.

"I don't know," he said. "I think I might be busy next Sunday." He glanced over to the doorway. Kevin was already gone.

"Anyway," he continued, "I'm not so sure Kevin wants to work with me."

Chapter 6

Isaac and Jackson studied the lineup for the night's game against the Orioles. As always, Coach Park had posted it on the dugout wall.

Giants v. Orioles—May 23

LF	Max Crosby	Reserves
2B	Caden Brandt	Liam Dorrien
SS	Ben Badillo	Ryan Aguilar
CF	Jared Jankowski	Elvis Campos
3B	Jackson Rhodes	
1B	Nate Webster	
RF	Isaac Burnett	
C	Alex Oquendo	
P	Charlie Anderson	

Isaac smacked the pocket of his glove with his fist. "I thought I'd be pitching tonight," he said to Jackson in a low voice.

"Coach is probably saving you for next week's game against the Rangers," Jackson suggested. "They're in first place. We're gonna need you against them."

Isaac looked at the fans gathering in the bleachers. He spotted his father talking to some of the other parents, but he kept searching the crowd.

"Yeah," Isaac said, "but I was hoping the T-bolts coach would be here and see me pitch against the Orioles. I could dominate those guys."

"Will you forget the T-bolts and think about the Giants? Coach is trying to figure out how *we* can win the most games." Jackson grabbed his glove. "Come on, let's warm up."

Isaac and Jackson tossed the ball back and forth. It was a great evening for baseball: cool, with just a hint of summer coming. Still, Isaac was finding it hard to get psyched up for the game. He couldn't help feeling jealous when he saw Charlie Anderson and Alex Oquendo warming up in the bullpen.

Isaac loved pitching—much more than he liked playing in the field or even batting. The pitcher controlled the game. He was in every play. Every pitch. After the game, the official scorer put a *W* for the win beside the pitcher's name. Not the right fielder. Not the shortstop. Just the pitcher.

Isaac steamed a fastball to Jackson. *The Orioles aren't that good,* he thought. *I could have thrown my perfect game tonight.*

"Bring it in!" Coach Park shouted. "You guys have seen the lineup. Charlie's pitching tonight. Make some plays for him." The coach nodded to the umpire and continued. "The Orioles are the home team, so we're up first. Max, Caden, and Ben are leading it off. Let's get some hits!"

Isaac slumped on the bench between Alex and Jackson. Coach Park seemed to sense Isaac's disappointment. He walked over, crouched down like a catcher, and looked him in the eye. "We're going to need you to pitch against the Rangers, Isaac." He patted him on the knee and added: "You've been pitching a lot. I don't want to use up my ace."

Coach walked away, clapping his hands and calling out encouragement to the batter. "Come on, Max! Good level swing. Start us off."

"See, I told you," Jackson said, leaning closer to Isaac. "He's saving you for the Rangers."

Isaac looked out at the field. "But I wanted to pitch against the Orioles. I could've owned them!"

"You'd beat the Orioles' butts, totally," Alex agreed.

"Hey, let's win *today*," Jackson said. "Then you'll beat the Rangers' butts—later."

The game with the Orioles went back and forth. The Giants grabbed a quick lead when Jackson knocked in two runs with a double. Isaac flew out to end the inning.

But the Orioles bounced back with two runs in the bottom of the second to tie the score, 2–2. Alex smashed a homer to put the

Giants ahead again, but the Orioles rallied with a run in the fifth.

Sitting on the bench, Isaac looked out at the scoreboard.

INNING	1	2	3	4	5	6
Giants	2	0	0	1	0	
Orioles	0	2	0	0	1	

The Giants and Orioles were tied 3–3 going into the sixth and final inning.

"Alex, warm up Liam!" Coach shouted. "He's going to pitch in the bottom of the inning. And Ryan, grab a bat. You're pinch-hitting. Let's get some base runners."

After Jared struck out looking, Jackson singled sharply up the middle. Now the Giants had a base runner and a chance to pull ahead!

A wild pitch skipped by Ryan's feet and Jackson advanced to second base. The Giants leaped off the bench, cheering at the top of their lungs.

"Come on, Ryan, bring him in!"

"Be a hitter!"

"Only takes one!"

Ryan slapped a pitch to left field. Jackson took off from second, rounded third, and ran like crazy for home, trying to beat the throw. Inches from the plate, Jackson glimpsed the ball coming in and dropped into a slide. The tip of his foot reached the base just as the catcher got the ball, bent over, and tagged him. The umpire hesitated a moment, then yelled, "Safe!"

The Giants were ahead, 4–3!

Two outs later, the Giants took the field clinging to a one-run lead. Isaac paced back and forth in right field cheering for Liam, but secretly wishing he could be on the mound to put the game away. "Come on, Liam, nothing but strikes! Work ahead. One-two-three inning."

Liam got the first two outs on a ground out and a pop-up. The Giants were just one out away from a hard-earned win.

"Come on, Liam, one more!" Isaac shouted. But Liam looked nervous. He walked the next Oriole on four shaky pitches. Runner on first, two outs. Isaac sensed real trouble after Liam fell behind the next batter—two balls, no strikes.

Crack! The Orioles batter smashed a line drive to right center field. Isaac raced over and cut off the ball before the fence. He knew that with two outs, there could be a play at the plate.

Isaac pivoted and fired a perfect one-hop throw to Alex at home. The Orioles runner put on the brakes and scrambled back to third base. Isaac's play had saved a run!

For the moment, at least. Now there were runners on second and third, and still two outs.

The Orioles batter lifted the next pitch high into right field. Isaac drifted over a few steps and caught the easy fly ball for the third out. The Giants had won, 4–3!

Jackson ran to high-five Isaac, and the two friends hustled off the field together. "See, your pitching arm helped us win even though you weren't on the mound," Jackson said. "That throw saved a run."

Isaac smiled and shrugged as the rest of the team celebrated.

"What a win!" Ben shouted.

"Put it there!" Caden shouted back, extending a victory fist bump to Ben.

"Good game, guys!" Coach Park yelled above the racket. "But we've got to play better against the Rangers." He pointed to Isaac. "Remember, you're pitching."

"Oh, yeah. I remember all right," Isaac said as he picked up his equipment bag and began stuffing his glove, bat, and jacket into it.

"Are you Isaac Burnett?" a woman's voice asked through the chain-link fence in back of the Giants bench.

Isaac looked up. He didn't recognize the woman. "Yeah, I'm Isaac."

"I'm Catherine Canavan. Coach Park told me your team was playing today. I'm Kevin's mother."

"Who?" Isaac slung his bag over his shoulder.

"Kevin. You played basketball with him on Sunday at Landmark School."

Isaac nodded. "Oh, yeah. The kid who stands by the door all the time."

Mrs. Canavan smiled. "That's Kevin. I wasn't there, but he told me he took some shots with you on Sunday."

"He talks?" Isaac was surprised at that news.

She laughed. "Kevin talks all the time. You just have to get him started. He's very shy." She looked over her shoulder. Isaac could see Kevin leaning against one of the bleacher poles the same way he leaned against the doorway at the gym. Mrs. Canavan turned back to Isaac. "Kevin wanted me to ask you whether you would be coming again on Sunday."

Isaac fumbled for the words. "I don't know...I mean...." He hadn't planned on going back.

"I think Kevin wants to take more shots with you." Mrs. Canavan leaned closer to the fence and lowered her voice. "It would be a big step for him."

"Just to take a few shots?" Isaac asked.

Kevin suddenly appeared beside his

mother. "I'm a shooter!" he declared in a too-loud voice. He leaped up as if he were taking a jump shot. "Swish—three in a row!"

Mrs. Canavan smiled at Isaac. "You can see how excited he is." She put her hand on Kevin's shoulder and looked at Isaac. "So will we see you Sunday?"

"Um...yeah, I guess so," Isaac said, glancing around the field and wondering if any of his Giants teammates were looking at him. He just wanted the conversation with Kevin and his mother to end.

"Great, see you then." Mrs. Canavan linked arms with her son and they started to leave.

Kevin turned suddenly. "See you Sunday. My game!" he shouted, pointing at his chest. Kevin hopped into the air, took another imaginary jump shot, and yelled, "Swish!"

Isaac heard the pounding basketballs before he heard the church bell chime twice. He rushed toward the gym and saw Kevin standing in the doorway. "You coming in?" Isaac asked. Kevin shook his head and looked away. It was as if the previous Sunday and the conversation at Isaac's baseball game had never happened.

Isaac walked over to Maya, who was rebounding for Theo and Phoenix. "What's with Kevin?" he asked. "I thought he'd be shooting around with everybody else."

"You have to be patient," Maya said. "It may take him a while."

Theo walked up to Isaac. His baseball hat was pushed back away from his round, smiling face. "Hi, I'm Theo," he said, putting out his hand. "What's your favorite movie?"

"What...? I don't...," Isaac stammered.

"Theo loves movies," Maya explained.

"My favorite's *Yellow Submarine*," Theo declared and began to sing the chorus of the song in his loudest voice.

"Come on, Theo," Maya said. "This is basketball practice, not music class."

"Give me the ball," Phoenix snapped. "I want to take my shots." He grabbed the ball and began to throw left-handed shots at the basket. His expression never changed, whether the ball went in the basket or bounced away.

Coach Park blew his whistle and Theo and Phoenix joined the other players gathering around him.

Isaac tried to coax Kevin away from the door. "Come on, buddy. Don't you want to—"

Before Isaac could get the question out of his mouth, Kevin turned toward the wall. Isaac looked over to the stands. Mrs. Canavan was sitting on the first row talking with another parent. Isaac couldn't figure out what was going on. He gave up and ran back to join the others. *I guess he doesn't want to play,* he thought.

After the players finished their warm-up exercises and drills, Coach Park pulled Isaac aside. "Why don't you take a ball to that side of the gym and see if you can get Kevin to take a few shots with you?"

"I tried," Isaac said. "I don't think he wants to."

Coach nudged him. "I know it looks that way, but you've got to be patient. Take it one step at a time. Go ahead, give it another try." He turned back to the group. "Okay, everybody against the wall. Start and Stop Whistle Drill."

Isaac dribbled slowly toward the door, switching between his right and left hands. "You want to take some shots?"

Kevin turned toward the wall again and clutched the doorjamb. He held on to it like a lifeline.

"Come on," Isaac said, faking a pass.

Kevin's hands didn't move an inch.

"Okay, have it your way." Isaac tossed in a shot at the closest basket. "See, it's easy," he said. "I can probably beat your record. What did you get? Three in a row?" Isaac felt like he was talking to himself.

The next shot bounced around the rim and fell through. Isaac grabbed the rebound and spun another shot off the backboard and through the net.

"That's three," Isaac declared. Another shot splashed through the net. "Four in a row!" He laughed. "I guess *I'm* the shooter now."

Isaac dribbled closer and faked another pass. This time Kevin's hands came up. Isaac saw that he was ready and bounced him a pass. Kevin didn't bobble it this time. And just like the previous Sunday, he took a couple of quick dribbles and tossed up a two-handed shot.

Swish!

"Four," Kevin said in a firm voice.

"What? Oh, I get it. You're counting the three from last time. That's cool," Isaac said as he flicked the ball to Kevin. "Keep it going."

Another shot. Another basket. "Five!" Kevin's voice rang out. He sounded almost excited.

Isaac put the ball on his hip and pointed to another spot on the floor. "You've gotta move around. You can't take the same shot every time," he said. "I've been shooting from different places on the floor."

Kevin took a few careful steps closer to the basket. His next shot rattled around the rim and fell in.

"Six!" he shouted.

"Good. Keep moving," Isaac reminded him. Kevin shifted to the side. His next shot thumped off the backboard and bounced away. His shoulders slumped and he started back to the doorway.

"Hey, wait, where are you going?" Isaac asked. "You can't hit *every* shot. Come on, nobody's perfect." Isaac motioned for the ball. "It's my turn. You rebound for me now."

"Okay," Kevin said with a half smile. "I'm a rebounder."

Isaac lined up his next shot. He wasn't sure whether to make it or miss it. Isaac lobbed the ball a little high. Air ball. He dropped his head and shoulders as if he were crushed by his missed shot.

"Nobody's perfect," Kevin said, echoing Isaac's words.

Isaac grinned. "Right. Okay, let's play best of five shots. You take the first turn."

The two boys played for a while, shooting, rebounding, and passing. They were in their own world as the other kids scrimmaged. While Kevin chased a missed pass, Isaac checked the action on the main court. Shontelle had just pushed a ball up into the big gray barrel. Danny was preparing to take a shot with his special green ball, working hard to balance himself without his crutches. Phoenix was yelling for the ball and Theo was running up and down the court, holding tight to his baseball cap so it wouldn't fall off.

"Want to play in the game?" Isaac asked Kevin.

Kevin shook his head. "I'm a shooter."

"How about shooting in a game?" Isaac suggested.

Coach Park blew his whistle. "Let's get in the circle."

Kevin didn't join the circle, but he didn't return to the doorway either. He stood with Isaac under the side basket, listening.

"Great practice," said Coach Park. "Everybody worked hard this afternoon. Good shooting, Phoenix. And Shontelle, that was a fantastic basket. Lucas and Theo, love the passing. We look like we're going to be ready for the big game in a few weeks."

As practice broke up, Kevin wandered over to the far end of the court and started shooting baskets by himself.

"You and Kevin were shooting up a storm today," Maya said to Isaac.

"Yeah, I tried to get him to play in the game, but no luck."

"Like I told you, you've got to be patient."

"What's this big game your dad was talking about?" Isaac asked.

"Oh, it's an exhibition game with Summit Hills School," Maya explained. "We play right here. It's not for a trophy or anything.

It's not as competitive as some Unified Sports games. We're more about practicing our skills and getting to play another school for the fun of it. And we do have fun. You'll see. This gym will look a lot different. There'll be cheerleaders and big homemade posters all over the walls. It's pretty cool."

"Has Kevin ever played in it?" Isaac asked.

"I don't think so," she said, checking her phone. "I've got to go. See you next week, right?"

"I'll be there," Isaac assured her. Then he turned and saw Mrs. Canavan walking toward him.

"Thank you," she said. "Kevin had fun today."

"He's a pretty good shooter," Isaac said as he watched Kevin sink another shot. "I tried to get him to play in the practice game, but he didn't want to."

Mrs. Canavan nodded as if she'd heard that before. "That's okay. You helped Kevin get away from the doorway. He was taking shots at the basket."

Isaac didn't know what to say.

Mrs. Canavan sensed his confusion. "Kevin's on the court, taking shots and having fun." She smiled. "That's huge."

ey, Jackson! Watch this." Isaac sped down the steep ramp on his skateboard, sailed across the flat surface, and bolted up another curved ramp. As the wheels of the skateboard flew above the second ramp, Isaac pivoted midair and pointed the front of the board back down the ramp.

In a flash he was sitting proudly beside Jackson on the ledge at the top of the first ramp. "How'd you like that?" he asked.

"Pretty good."

"P-pretty good?" Isaac sputtered. "That was a perfect 180-degree turn! As good as...who's that hotshot skateboard guy? Tony something?"

"Tony Hawk," someone said.

Isaac and Jackson whipped around to see Maya dribbling a basketball toward them. "I thought I saw you guys when I was shooting baskets. What are a couple of big-time baseball players doing here?"

"Just messing around," Isaac said. "But if we get hurt, Coach will be furious. We've got a big game tomorrow."

"I know, against the Rangers. My dad's been talking about it for days." Maya smiled and pointed at the skateboard. "Can I try?"

"Sure. Take my helmet."

Maya put it on and tightened the chin strap. "Here goes nothing," she said. Maya zipped down the ramp and began cruising through the course. She didn't have any fancy tricks, but she didn't fall either.

Jackson turned to Isaac. "Who's she?"

"Coach Park's daughter, Maya," Isaac said and then smiled. "So you'd better be nice to her or he'll bench you."

"How do you know her?"

"She helps out with that Sunday basketball team I told you about."

"You mean the retarded kids?"

"Yeah," Isaac said, "but don't use that word in front of Maya. She doesn't like it. She says it's mean." He didn't feel like talking about the basketball team, so he turned to watch Maya. When she finished the course, she came over and plopped down between Isaac and Jackson.

"Nice job," Isaac said. "You're a regular female Tony Hawk."

Maya rolled her eyes. "I was just trying to get around the course without breaking my neck." Then she changed the subject. "So are you guys ready for your big game against the Rangers?"

"We've got Isaac on the bump," Jackson said. "So we're ready."

"Yeah, my dad says he does a really good job pitching." Maya turned to Isaac. "You're doing a really good job with Kevin too."

"Who's Kevin?" Jackson asked.

"One of the Special Olympics kids," Isaac said quickly.

"Kevin used to stand in the doorway of the gym just watching," Maya explained.

"Now Isaac has him shooting like a pro."

"Cool," Jackson said.

"It's not that big a deal," Isaac protested. "I mean, it's not like he's ever going to light it up in a real game."

"*Real* game?" Maya sounded annoyed. "What? His games aren't real? But your games are?"

"Yeah, um, no...I mean...."

Maya looked out toward the sunset and the baseball diamond where the Giants played their games. "Where do you pitch from in your games?" she asked.

"The pitcher's mound."

"No, I mean how far away from home plate?"

"Fifty-two feet...in our league. We're the twelve- and thirteen-year—"

Maya cut Isaac off. "In a *real* game, the pitcher has to pitch from 60 feet, 6 inches, right?"

"Yeah, but—"

"What kind of bats do you use?" Maya asked.

Jackson jumped in. "Aluminum," he said.

"That's why they had to make the outfield fence higher. The ball really jumps off the—"

"Pros use wood bats," Maya said, her voice getting tighter. "In *real* games."

"Okay, okay." Isaac tried not to sound too upset. "I'll admit we don't do everything the same way the pros do. But we will someday. You know that Kevin's never gonna be a really good player."

"Chances are you're never going to play in the major leagues, Isaac. So why do you bother playing baseball now?"

"What's that supposed to mean?" Isaac didn't wait for an answer. "I like playing baseball. And I'm pretty good at it."

"Yeah, well, Theo, Shontelle, and Phoenix like playing basketball. Did you see Theo dancing around after he scored a basket last Sunday?"

Now Isaac wished Maya hadn't barged in on Jackson and him.

She seemed to sense Isaac's frustration. "Look, Isaac," she said in a softer voice, "the Sunday basketball kids aren't trying to be perfect. They have fun. They work really hard even though basketball isn't easy for them. They keep at it. And they're getting better! That's *perfect enough* for me."

"All right, all right. They're perfect enough." Isaac wanted to change the subject, but Jackson beat him to it.

"Are you coming to our game against the Rangers?" he asked Maya.

She thought for a moment. The sun had dipped below the trees and the horizon was fiery red. "Maybe I will," she said, glancing at Isaac. "And see how good you guys really are."

Isaac sat on the Giants bench, his legs stretched out in front of him. He checked the scoreboard and smiled.

INNING	1	2	3	4	5	6
Giants	0	0	1	1	0	
Rangers	0	0	0	0	0	

After five innings, the Giants led the Rangers, 2–0. So far Isaac's pitching had been perfect. Against the best team in the league. No runs, no hits, no errors, no walks, no base runners.

His teammates crowded together at the other end of the dugout. Even Jackson wouldn't come near him for fear of jinxing his perfect game.

"Caden, Ben, and Jared are up this inning," Coach Park called. "Let's get some hits. We need some more runs."

That's just Coach talking, Isaac thought. *We don't need any more runs. The way I'm pitching, the Rangers will be lucky to get on base.*

This was the game Isaac had dreamed of a thousand times. Dreamed of in his backyard. In his bedroom. At school.

None of the batters had gotten a good swing at anything he was throwing today.

After just the first inning, Alex had said, "Man, you've got it going today. Even the Rangers can't touch you." Alex hadn't said much to him after that. In fact, the team had barely said a word to Isaac since Ben, the Giants shortstop, had made a nice running catch on a pop-up to end the fourth. The team could feel it. This could be the one. And now Isaac was three outs from a perfect game!

The Giants added another run with a walk and two singles in the top of the sixth. So Isaac had a 3–0 cushion when he stepped confidently onto the mound in the sixth and final inning.

Coach Park was pumped up and pacing. "Come on. One-two-three inning. Tight defense. Let's make a play for him. Nothing gets through."

Coach and the Giants defense didn't have to worry about the first Rangers batter. Isaac zipped three straight fastballs by him for an easy out.

The Giants infielders tossed the ball "around the horn" and cheered Isaac on as the next Rangers hitter stepped into the batter's box.

"One down, two to go."

"Nothing but strikes, Isaac! Nothing but strikes!"

"No batter, no batter."

Jackson tossed the ball in to Isaac, who quickly turned toward the plate and sized up the situation. *Two more batters,* he thought. *Bottom of the order. Hello, perfect game!*

Sure enough, he blazed the first pitch by the Rangers batter.

Strike one.

Alex signaled for another fastball.

Isaac nodded. *No way this kid is catching up to my fastball.* He wound up and threw the ball with everything he had. The Rangers player flicked his bat across home plate, slicing a blooper toward short right field. Nate Webster, the Giants first baseman, froze for an instant, not sure whether to jump and try to snag the ball in midflight or race back and let the ball drop into his glove. By the time Nate started to run back, it was too late. The ball was beyond his reach. It floated over his head and landed just inches inside the foul line in the outfield grass for a base hit.

The entire Rangers bench exploded in cheers and loud clapping.

Isaac couldn't believe it! One lucky Rangers hit and his perfect game was gone!

Steaming mad, he smoked three straight fastballs past the Rangers number nine hitter for the second out of the inning. The next batter sent a lazy fly to center field. Isaac was already walking off the mound when the ball settled into Jared's glove for the final out. He hardly listened as Coach Park congratulated the Giants on the big 3–0 win and reminded them of their upcoming practice and next game.

Isaac was shoving his baseball gear into his bag when he heard a familiar voice. "Almost, champ." He looked around and saw his father standing right beside him.

"I was *so* close," Isaac said as he yanked too hard on the zipper of his bag. "That was such a dumb hit. Nate should've had it." Isaac could feel his voice getting louder, but he didn't care who heard him.

"Settle down," his dad said. "You did great. A game like that'll help you make the Thunderbolts."

"Was the coach here?" Isaac stopped what he was doing. "Did you see him?"

Mr. Burnett shook his head. "No, but he's got to hear about a one-hitter. Especially against the Rangers."

"I guess so." Isaac finished zipping his bag and handed it to his dad. "Can you take this? I've got my skateboard."

"Okay. See you at home." His father waved as he walked away.

Isaac's skateboard was under the bench, but he sat down to take a few minutes just to think.

Coach Park came over to where he was sitting. Maya was following close behind him. "Good win," Coach said. "We really needed that one."

"I guess Jackson was right," Maya admitted. "You are pretty good on the bump. You almost had a no-hitter."

"I almost had a *perfect game*," Isaac corrected Maya. He could feel the impatience in his voice. But he was glad that he had shown her he was a real pitcher. Pitching in a real game.

"The most important thing is that we got the win," Coach said. "I've already updated the league standings. Here, you want to take a look?"

Coach handed Isaac his phone.

Team	Record	Games Behind
Rangers	10–1	—
Nationals	8–3	2
Giants	8–3	2
Yankees	6–5	4
Pirates	6–5	4
Rockies	3–8	7
Royals	2–9	8
Orioles	1–10	9

Isaac was still fuming. "Can you believe that lucky hit in the last inning?" he said, barely looking at the standings.

"Don't worry about that. Wins are more important," Coach said.

Yeah, Isaac thought, *but a perfect game is a perfect win.*

The Giants coach stared at Isaac for a moment, studying his star pitcher. "Ever heard of Philip Humber? Dallas Braden?

"Not really."

"They both pitched perfect games, and not that long ago," Coach said. "How about Len Barker?"

Isaac shook his head.

"He pitched a perfect game too," Coach said. "Charlie Robertson?"

Isaac was beginning to catch on. "He pitched a perfect game?"

Coach nodded. "None of those guys had winning records for their careers, but they all pitched perfect games. Don Larsen—the guy who pitched the only perfect game in a World Series—didn't have a winning record either."

"Yeah, but my dad said some great pitchers had perfect games too," Isaac argued. "Koufax...Randy Johnson...I think even Cy Young threw one."

"But they weren't great just because they pitched one perfect game," Coach Park insisted. "They were great because they won a lot of games. A good pitcher gives his team a chance to win, like you did today." Coach Park clapped Isaac on his shoulder as he turned to go. "Just keep getting better. Perfect games are a lot about luck. Don't worry about being perfect."

"Yeah. Just be perfect enough," Maya

added with a funny little smile.

Isaac rolled his eyes, but smiled a little too.

Her father looked confused. "What are you guys talking about?"

"Nothing, Dad." Maya said, still smiling. "Will we see you Sunday?"

Isaac thought for a moment before answering. "Yeah. I'll be there."

saac raced into the Landmark gym and looked around the floor. The scene was the same as always for practices. Phoenix was tossing shots at a side basket. Danny was trying to loft his special green ball up toward a basket as Bella and Avi made sure he kept his balance without his crutches. Theo was shaking hands with parents in the bleachers—again.

The only thing that was different was Kevin. He wasn't hanging out in the doorway. He was on the floor, taking shot after shot at the far end of the gym! No one was rebounding for him, so when the ball bounced away he chased it, turned, and tossed up another two-handed shot.

Isaac saw Maya coming toward him, pushing Shontelle in her wheelchair. He couldn't wait to announce the good news. "Kevin's—"

Maya didn't let him finish. "Yeah, he came right in today, grabbed a basketball, and started shooting." Maya shook her head in disbelief. "I tried to rebound for him, but he didn't seem to want me around. So I thought Shontelle and I should work together. Right, girlfriend?" Maya and Shontelle exchanged a high five.

"Maybe I'll try rebounding for him," Isaac said. "See you guys later." He slipped past the other players and jogged over to where Kevin was playing.

He watched as Kevin tossed up a corner jumper that bounced off the rim. Kevin retrieved the ball quickly and hurled another shot.

Swish!

"Great shot," Isaac said. "Need a rebounder?"

Kevin almost smiled. "You're a rebounder," he said. "I'm a shooter."

"Okay," Isaac agreed. "But you've got to rebound for me too."

The two boys kept shooting until Coach Park blew his whistle to start practice. "Let's all get in a big circle."

Before Isaac could say a word, Kevin stepped toward the team circle. Not all the way, but close enough that Lucas was able to grab him and give him a hug. Kevin wriggled free and inched back a few steps.

"Okay, listen up everybody. Let's do some stretches," Coach Park said. "Reach as high as you can."

Isaac tried to nudge Kevin closer into the circle, but he stayed stubbornly where he was, rubbing his hands on the sides of his legs.

"Come on, Kevin!" barked Phoenix. "Stretch it out! Stretch it out!"

Kevin didn't move.

After the warm-up, Coach Park announced the Start and Stop Whistle Drill and everybody headed for the wall. Well, almost everybody. Kevin headed for the sidelines, sat on the floor, and pulled his knees up to his chin. He rocked gently back and forth and peered out over the tops of his knees.

Coach Park called to him. "Kevin, you want to—"

"No," Kevin answered in a clear voice.

"He's never done that either," Maya whispered to Isaac. "I don't think he's ever said one word to my dad."

After the team finished their drills, Coach Park pulled Isaac aside. "Why don't you practice with the team today?" he suggested. "Maybe that'll get Kevin out on the court."

So Isaac did. But Coach's plan didn't work.

Kevin just sat there and watched everyone, his eyes darting back and forth. After a few minutes he got up and started taking shots at a side basket. Alone.

Isaac stopped worrying about Kevin and got into the scrimmage. He passed to Theo for a layup. Theo made it easily, straightened his baseball hat, and pointed to Isaac like a pro.

"Hey, Isaac!" Phoenix shouted. "Why don't you pass one to me?"

When it was Shontelle's turn for a shot, Isaac ran over with Avi and grabbed the big gray barrel. They held it up close to her.

"Come on, you can do it!" Isaac urged. "Just a little harder, a little higher. Nice basket!"

Isaac shot a glance at Kevin and caught him watching the game. But after a few seconds, Kevin went back to shooting.

"Isaac!" Coach yelled. "Get Danny's green ball. Let's give him a few shots."

Grabbing the ball from the sidelines, Isaac dribbled to the basket. The ball was so light and lively, it almost bounced away from him. Danny put down his crutches as Isaac handed him the ball.

Coach Park stood under the basket, urging Danny on. "Get two hands underneath the ball. Try to bend your legs as much as you can and push up. Hard as you can!"

Danny looked up at the basket. It was only ten feet high, but it must have seemed a million miles away to him.

His first shot floated maybe seven feet above the floor, fell softly, and rolled away. Isaac retrieved the ball and handed it to Danny. The second shot was closer. The third almost hit the rim. Danny's face was a mask of determination and effort.

He took a few more shots. He didn't make any baskets, but there was lots of cheering. Even Phoenix joined in.

"Come on, Danny, you can do it!"

"Only takes one."

"He stops, he pops!"

After another shot had fallen short, Coach Park grabbed the green ball. "Great job, Danny," he said. "You're doing a whole lot better."

Smiling, Danny traded high fives with his teammates.

Coach Park clapped his hands to get everyone's attention. "Let's switch up teams!" he shouted. "Five minutes for a quick scrimmage. How about Isaac, Phoenix, Danny, and...let's see." He looked around. "Maya, Shontelle, and...Kevin."

Kevin stepped up to join the team. Isaac

and Maya looked at each other wide-eyed, as if they'd just seen a winning basket or a game-ending home run. But they stayed quiet.

When the scrimmage started, Kevin raced up and down the court from baseline to baseline, hardly paying attention to his teammates and the ball. He clapped his hands and put them up high on defense. It was as if he had been saving up his energy all these weeks in order to play today.

Isaac got the ball and passed it to Kevin, who tossed a shot up from almost half court. The ball slammed against the backboard with a loud smack and bounced away.

"Try to get a little closer next time, Kevin," Coach Park suggested.

"Pass it to me, will ya?" Phoenix shouted.

As Maya wheeled Shontelle past Isaac, she leaned over and said, "Kevin's officially part of the team now. Phoenix is yelling at him."

Isaac laughed.

Coach blew his whistle. "Circle up!"

Kevin dashed back to the sidelines, sat

on the floor in his curled-up position, and began rocking again.

"I wish he'd come over to the circle," Isaac said to Maya.

Maya pushed Shontelle's chair into the circle. "Don't worry," she said. "Kevin's already done a lot today. And look...."

Kevin's knees were still pulled up near his chin, but Isaac could see that he was smiling.

"See how happy he is?" Maya whispered.

Come on," Isaac's dad said, tossing him his glove. "Let's go. We've got some work to do."

Isaac pushed open the back door and stepped into the yard. Although it was after dinner, a soft spring light lingered. The days were getting longer. A promise of summer was in the air.

"We've still got plenty of light," Mr. Burnett said, looking at the sky. "That's good. Last game I noticed a few things you need to work on." Instead of moving toward their backyard home plate, he followed Isaac to the mound. "Your fastball was getting away from you in your game against the Pirates," he said. "I think you were opening up your shoulder too much."

"I threw okay." Isaac turned to face his dad. "We got the win, 6–3." Before his father could respond, Isaac added, "And I threw a one-hitter the game before that. Against the Rangers, remember? And that was just a lucky hit."

"Maybe so, but it was still a hit."

"But Dad—"

His father didn't let up. "And the Pirates got a lot more than one hit off you. They must have gotten seven or eight. So we have to work on your release point for your fastball."

Isaac didn't say anything, so his father kept talking. "I thought you were the guy who wanted to pitch a *perfect* game, Isaac. You do that and you're a cinch to make the Thunderbolts."

"Yeah, I know. But—"

"Okay, let's see you go through your pitching motion real slow."

Isaac obeyed, beginning to throw an imaginary pitch in slow motion.

"Stop right there," Mr. Burnett said just as Isaac's arm swung above his head.

Isaac froze in place.

His dad stepped closer and moved Isaac's arm and hand slightly to the right.

Isaac felt himself tighten.

"Come on, loosen up," his father said. "You want to let go of your fastball a little bit more to the side. I think you were coming over the top too much."

"It feels funny," Isaac said.

"You'll get used to it," his father said.

"I hope so," Isaac said. Then he asked, "Do you really think this will help?"

"Yeah, I do." Isaac's father walked toward the plate at the other side of the yard. "Let's throw a few to warm up."

They threw back and forth for a minute.

"How many kids make the Thunder-bolts?" Mr. Burnett asked, tossing the ball to Isaac.

"About fifteen. They invite twenty-five or thirty kids to try out."

"How many pitchers?"

"I don't know. Six or seven, I guess."

"Yeah, but remember, lots of the other pitchers can play other positions," Isaac's father said, snagging a throw. "You'll have to make it as a pitcher."

"I can play the field!" Isaac said. "I'm a pretty good outfielder."

"Maybe in a pinch. But they aren't going to pick you to play the outfield." Mr. Burnett tossed the ball back to Isaac. "Keep your shoulder in on every throw. Watch." His dad went through a pitching motion very slowly.

Isaac's mother leaned out the back door. "Isaac, your phone is buzzing."

He started for the door, but his father stopped him. "You can check it later. We'd better work on that fastball. There's not much light left."

Isaac looked at his mother, shrugged his shoulders, and stepped back toward the pitching rubber. "You want me to throw some pitches?"

"Sure. Remember what I showed you about your release point."

Isaac nodded. The first few pitches felt pretty good and zipped straight to his father's glove. Then two sailed high and wide.

Isaac's father marched across the backyard again. He took Isaac's arm and forced it into the position he had showed him earlier. "I want you to get your arm to this spot every time," he said, a bit of impatience leaking into his voice.

"It still feels funny, Dad."

"I'm telling you, you'll get used to it."

"What about other kinds of pitches?" Isaac asked as his father walked away.

"Just fastballs today. I want you to be able to spot your fastball better."

As the two returned to their game, a strange quiet fell over the backyard. The only sounds were Mr. Burnett's calls— "Strike" or "Ball"—and the smack of the ball against the leather of the baseball gloves. All the other baseball talk had faded in the twilight.

Isaac tried his best to concentrate on his release point on every pitch. Most of the time his pitches flew right to their target. But sometimes they trailed out of the strike zone. When that happened, he tried to keep himself focused on his pitching, but it was hard. His dad had taken all the fun out of it.

As the daylight melted away, Isaac's mind drifted back to the most recent Unified Sports basketball practice. Kevin had played more than ever before. In his mind, Isaac could see the Sunday athletes—Theo, Phoenix, Shontelle, Lucas, Danny, and especially Kevin—hustling up and down the court the best they could, shouting, clapping, working on their games. They didn't do everything perfectly, but they loved playing.

His father's voice disturbed Isaac's daydream. "You're opening up your shoulder again!" he shouted as he tossed the ball back to Isaac. "That's why the ball's moving up and out of the strike zone."

Isaac went into his windup and threw hard to the plate. The ball sailed high. Isaac's dad flicked it out of the air with a flash of his glove. Without a word, he popped up from his catcher's crouch and moved toward the mound again.

Isaac's shoulders slumped. "I was only off on a couple of pitches, Dad," he said. "I don't have to be perfect on every pitch."

"Look, do you want to make the Thunderbolts or what?" When his father was only a few feet away, he added—as Isaac knew he would—"Practice doesn't make perfect; *perfect* practice makes perfect."

The sun ducked behind the trees and houses. The wind kicked up, chasing away the warmth of the day.

Chapter 12

The next evening, Isaac steered his skateboard through his neighborhood streets. The Giants didn't have a game or practice. He'd finished his homework. And his father was working late.

That was okay with Isaac. He needed time to think.

The tryouts for the T-bolts were coming up soon, and Isaac still wanted to make the team.

The Giants had one more game to play before the season was over, and Isaac still wanted to pitch a perfect game.

But the pressure was getting to him. The pressure from his dad. The pressure he put on himself. It was like nothing was ever good enough. Not even a one-hitter against the Rangers or a pitch less than an inch off the outside corner of the plate.

It wasn't like Sunday basketball, where everyone cheered for every shot no matter whether the ball went in the basket or not. Where everybody seemed to be happy to play and do their best.

Isaac zoomed down a steep sidewalk. The wind and sun felt good on his face. He slipped his right foot off the board and pushed up the next hill. He didn't feel like doing tricks, so he decided not to go to the skateboard park and turned toward Crocker Park instead.

When he arrived, he coasted to a stop and flipped his board up into his hand. He looked out over the park. The high school baseball field was empty. The score from that afternoon was still up on the board. A couple of kids with lacrosse sticks ran across the outfield grass, chucking a ball back and forth. Two women volleyed on one of the tennis courts.

In the distance, a kid was shooting baskets by himself. As Isaac watched the solitary figure toss shot after shot at the backboard, he realized the kid's loose-limbed, two-handed shot looked familiar.

"Hi there," a woman called from a bench overlooking the park. It was Mrs. Canavan.

"Hi," Isaac answered. "Is that Kevin shooting baskets down there?"

"Yeah, he's been practicing."

Isaac watched Kevin sink a long one. "He's getting pretty good."

"I'm a shooter," Mrs. Canavan said, making her voice sound like her son's.

Isaac laughed. A question bubbled up inside him—something he'd wanted to ask for a while. "What's Kevin got?" he started. "I mean, you know, what's wrong with him? Nobody's ever told me. I'm just, you know, curious."

Mrs. Canavan stared straight ahead. She seemed to be looking past the basketball court, past her son, to some other time and place. "It's called fragile X syndrome," she said, turning toward Isaac. "It's genetic.

Kevin was born with it. Mostly it means he's developmentally behind other kids intellectually, socially. And in a lot of other ways."

She looked over at Isaac. "How old are you?"

"Thirteen. I'll be fourteen in the fall."

"Kevin's fourteen, he'll be fifteen in November," she said. "But he only reads on a second-grade level."

"He reads?" Isaac asked, surprised. "I didn't know that."

"Oh, yes. Kevin loves to read." Mrs. Canavan smiled. "He and his dad go over the sports news together every morning. We got him some wonderful tutors and so he's doing very well, but...." She swept her hair away from her face. She didn't sound upset, just tired. "Kevin can do a lot of things. But nothing comes easily for him. Everything will always be a struggle."

"Like when Shontelle makes a basket?" Isaac pictured the girl in her wheelchair, pushing the basketball up the side of the big gray barrel.

Mrs. Canavan nodded. "Or when Danny tries to." She watched as Kevin eyed the net, preparing for another shot. "You know what I love about our Sunday kids? They don't give up. And the smallest thing can make them feel proud and happy. Making a basket. Or just playing." She smiled as Kevin's shot went in. "He's never going to be the best at anything. He's never going to get it perfect. But he's happy when he does something better than he's done it before."

Isaac watched Kevin chase a missed shot to the corner, take a quick dribble, and shoot again. Another miss and Kevin was chasing the ball again.

"Is he practicing for that big exhibition game? The one they play against the other Unified Sports team?" Isaac asked. "Will he play in that?"

Mrs. Canavan shrugged. "I'm not sure. It's a big crowd, lots of noise. I don't know if he can handle that. Kevin is very shy. Like lots of kids with fragile X syndrome, he gets anxious around people he doesn't know." She smiled. "He's not like Theo."

Isaac laughed, thinking about the big kid and his Nationals hat. "Theo will probably give a speech at the game."

"Do you know Theo is a greeter at the YMCA?"

"Really?"

"Yeah, he says hi to everyone who comes in," she said. "He's great at it."

Isaac thought for a moment. "You should bring Kevin to our next game. It's our last one," he said. "We're playing the Rockies. I'm pitching. It might help him get used to crowds and stuff."

"Okay. That would be fun for him." She leaned back on the bench, gazing at her son on the court. "You know, Isaac," she said as Kevin hit a three-pointer, "he might play in that big game if you're there."

Isaac thought for a moment, then put his skateboard down next to her. "Will you watch this for a while?"

"Where are you going?"

"I thought I'd take some shots with Kevin."

"Sure," Mrs. Canavan said, pulling the

skateboard a little closer. "He'll like that."

Isaac trotted off past the lacrosse players. When he stepped onto the basketball court, he held his hands out for a pass. "Hey, teammate, give me the ball. I'm open."

Kevin bounced Isaac a pass without hesitating. Isaac's shot rattled around the loose metal rim and fell through the chain net. Kevin grabbed the ball and turned to take a shot.

Isaac stopped him. "Hey!" he shouted, reaching out for the ball again. "How about some courtesy?"

"Curtsy?" Kevin's face twisted into a question.

"Cour-te-sy," Isaac said, sounding out the word for him. "I made my last shot, so I get another one. It's called courtesy. You get courtesy on any playground in America."

"Okay, cour-te-sy," Kevin repeated carefully and tossed Isaac a pass. Isaac's shot bounced away and he began rebounding for Kevin.

"Cour-te-sy!" Kevin shouted after his

first shot splashed through the net.

"Are you going to play in the big game?" Isaac asked as he bounced him a pass.

Kevin stood stone still for a moment, poised to shoot. He seemed to be thinking hard before he answered.

"Maybe," he muttered, then lofted the ball in a high arc straight into the basket.

Chapter **13**

It was the top of the fifth.

The Giants' last game.

And things weren't going well. The Rockies had scored two runs off of Isaac in the second inning and two in the third. But he was hanging in there.

A lot of people had come to see him pitch. Kevin was there with his mom and dad. Maya too. And Mr. Dorsett, the T-bolts coach, was sitting two rows in back of Isaac's parents.

Isaac didn't want to give up and get pulled from the mound. He could still win this one...if he kept his head in the game.

The Rockies were ahead, 4–2, with runners on second and third.

Isaac took a deep breath and narrowed his gaze at the batter. *I got two strikes on him. Just need one more.*

"Come on, Isaac. Bear down!" Coach Park called. "Get this guy."

Isaac wound up and whistled a fastball toward the plate. The Rockies batter took a big cut. And missed.

Strike three!

Isaac let out a deep breath. *Two outs,* he thought. *Crunch time. I gotta get this next guy.* He started with a changeup.

Crack!

Isaac spun to see Jared drift back for the easy catch. The Giants were still behind by two runs, but they had two more turns at bat to make something happen.

Isaac sat down on the bench beside Mrs. Badillo, Ben's mother, who was keeping the score book for the team. "Can I see my pitching stats?" he asked.

She handed him the score book, and Isaac studied the neat columns of figures.

INNING	PITCHES	STRIKES	BALLS	RUNS
1st	卌卌丨 ⑪	卌丨丨丨 ⑧	丨丨丨 ③	0
2nd	卌卌卌丨 ⑯	卌卌 ⑩	卌丨 ⑥	2
3rd	卌卌丨丨丨 ⑭	卌丨丨丨丨 ⑨	卌 ⑤	2
4th	卌卌 ⑩	卌丨丨丨 ⑧	丨丨 ②	0
5th	卌卌卌丨丨 ⑰	卌卌 ⑩	卌丨丨 ⑦	0
6th				

"Your teammates haven't helped you much," she said, looking over his shoulder. "Two errors, and a couple of plays we should have made."

"Yeah. And the Rockies had some lucky hits," Isaac added. "Nothing's been easy."

He wished the T-bolts coach hadn't come to this game. *Four runs in five innings,* Isaac thought. *If only he'd come to my one-hitter.*

"Go, Giants!" Kevin's voice was clear above the noise of the crowd.

Isaac's mind flashed back to the Sunday basketball games. Kevin stepping away from the doorway. Shontelle pushing the ball up the side of the barrel. Danny shooting the lightweight green ball closer and closer to the 10-foot basket.

Isaac punched his glove and gave himself a quick pep talk. *All right, it doesn't have to be a perfect game. Just hang in there. Give your team a chance to win. That's what good pitchers do.*

The Giants squeezed out another run on a two-out hit by Jared. They only trailed by one run when they ran back out onto the field.

Coach Park grabbed Isaac by the arm. "Throw strikes. Work hard, keep it close."

But Isaac's streak of bad luck continued. The first Rockies batter tapped a slow roller down the third-base line. Jackson charged the ball.

"Let it go!" Alex yelled, ripping off his catcher's mask. Isaac, Jackson, and Alex surrounded the ball, willing it to go foul. But it stopped inches inside the baseline. Fair ball. The Rockies had a runner on first, no outs.

The second batter slapped a ground ball

to shortstop. *Double play!* Isaac thought as he whirled around. But the ball took a funny hop and bounced off Ben's glove. Both runners were safe.

Man, we can't get a break today, Isaac thought as he faced the next hitter.

The batter placed a sacrifice bunt down the third-base line. Jackson's only play was to first base. One out. Runners on second and third.

The next batter popped the ball straight up. Alex caught it right in front of the backstop. Two outs. Isaac and the Giants just needed one more to finish the inning.

Isaac blistered two fastballs by the batter to get in front of the count. No balls. Two strikes. Isaac's next pitch cut the heart of the plate.

Crack! The ball rocketed back to Isaac and he knocked it down with his glove. He scrambled after it, then fired to first from his knees, beating the runner by half a step.

"Great play!" Jackson said as the team headed into the dugout.

"It wasn't pretty." Isaac smiled, remembering how he'd crawled after the ball. "But

I got him." The Giants still trailed by one run, 4–3.

Coach Park clapped his hands. "Come on, guys," he said. "Last ups: Jackson, Liam, and Alex. Isaac's up after that. We need base runners."

The Giants got their base runners as Jackson smacked a single to left and Liam worked a walk. Runners on first and second, no outs.

Alex tried to bunt, but popped up to the pitcher. Isaac stepped to the plate with two on and one out. The Giants and their fans were on their feet.

"Be a hitter, Isaac!"

"Only takes one."

"Make it be in there."

Isaac smacked a bouncer right at the Rockies shortstop. *Oh no! Double-play ball!* he thought, but he bolted from the batter's box and sprinted full speed to first base. The shortstop ran in, touched second for the force-out, and fired to first. Isaac's foot touched the bag a split second before the throw from second smacked into the first baseman's mitt.

Safe!

The Giants were still alive. Runners at first and third, two outs. "Run on anything!" Coach Park reminded Isaac and Jackson.

Crack! Max drove the ball deep into left center field. Isaac was off and running. As he rounded second, he could tell from the roar of the crowd that Jackson had crossed home with the tying run. Now it was up to Isaac to win the game! He glanced to the outfield. The Rockies were still chasing the ball. Then he spotted Coach Park at third base, wind-milling his arm, sending him all the way home! Isaac turned on the speed. He was really flying now and the crowd was going crazy.

Isaac slid into home with time to spare and popped up ready to celebrate with his teammates, who started rushing toward him. The team quickly became one big happy circle, full of chest bumps and high fives.

The Giants had won, 5–4!

The celebration finally ended and everyone went to gather their stuff.

Isaac's father gave him a pat on the back. "Tough game," he said.

"Dad, we won," Isaac reminded him. "I'm happy about that."

"Yeah, me too," his father admitted.

His mother gave him a hug. "Great baserunning, Isaac! I got so nervous in that last inning I couldn't watch!"

"I know, Mom. But close games are really fun!"

She smiled. "We'll see you at home," she said as she headed toward the car with his dad.

Isaac was taking a swig from his water bottle when Kevin came over and stood with his hand up, ready for a high five.

"Hey, Kevin!" Isaac slapped his hand and smiled.

"You're a pitcher!" Kevin shouted.

"And a base runner!" Isaac laughed.

Kevin tapped his chest with his finger. "*My* game next."

Isaac traded looks with Kevin's mom. The way she tilted her head made Isaac think that she was hoping her son might play in the big game on Sunday. But Isaac knew you could never be 100 percent sure with Kevin.

After the Canavans walked away, Isaac tossed his glove in his equipment bag and zipped it shut.

"Was that the retarded kid you play basketball with?" Jackson asked, coming over to get his water bottle on the bench.

"Hey, lose that word, Jackson," Isaac snapped. "It's so mean! Really!"

"Sorry, man."

"He has a name! It's Kevin. And he's a good guy."

"I said I was sorry." Jackson changed the subject quickly. "Hey, thanks for getting the Giants another win." The two boys traded soft fist bumps. "I gotta run."

"Good game," a voice said. Isaac looked up. It was Mr. Dorsett, the Thunderbolts coach.

"It wasn't my best game," Isaac said quickly. "Not even close." He felt nervous in front of Mr. Dorsett, but kept talking. "I wish you could've seen me pitch against the

Rangers. I threw a one-hitter, almost a perfect game."

Mr. Dorsett nodded. "I heard about that game. But I liked what I saw out there today. You battled. You didn't give up."

Isaac didn't know what to say, so he just listened.

"The Thunderbolts play a lot of good teams. We're going to need pitchers who don't give up. We want guys on the mound who give their team a chance to win." The coach smiled. "I hope you're going to try out."

"What? I mean *when*...um...when are the tryouts?"

"Next Saturday. Right here. One o'clock."

Coach Dorsett didn't have to tell him twice. This time Isaac knew exactly what to say.

"I'll be there."

Chapter 14

Isaac heard the music before anything else. A fast, thumping bass line spilled into the hallway. He zigzagged his way through a clump of parents and kids jammed around the door and slipped into the Landmark gym.

The scene was completely different from Sunday practices. The players were warming up the way they usually did, but the place was packed with spectators. A group of cheerleaders in matching blue shirts were whipping up the crowd. A boy in a wheelchair pumped his pom-poms to the beat. The whole gym was pulsing with excitement.

Neon-colored posters covered the walls:

Go Landmark Lions!

Go Summit Hills Dolphins!

You Can Do It Theo!!!

Score a Basket!!!

WE LOVE YOU SHONTELLE!

Isaac looked around for Kevin. He didn't see him anywhere. He spotted Maya and shouted over the music, "Have you seen Kevin?"

Maya bounced a ball to Theo, who tossed a shot at the basket. "I thought I saw him earlier!" she said loud enough for Isaac to hear. "He must be around here somewhere."

As Isaac circled the gym searching for Kevin, the music stopped and a woman's voice blared out of the loudspeakers. "I want to welcome everyone to the Eighth Annual

Special Olympics Unified Sports Basketball Exhibition between the Landmark Lions and the Summit Hills Dolphins!" The crowd applauded and the cheerleaders danced and shook their pom-poms.

Coach Park quickly gathered his players around him. When the noise died down a little, he started calling out instructions. "Okay, Lions. Listen to me. I want the following kids to pair up. I will introduce you together and then you'll run out onto the floor. Phoenix and Bella, Shontelle and Maya, Theo and Avi...Avi, go get Theo. He's in the stands talking to the parents—"

Isaac caught Coach Park's eye. "Where's Kevin?" he shouted over the music and cheering.

"I don't know," Coach Park said, raising his voice to be heard. "I saw him come in with his mom. Why don't you try to find him? You're going to be his partner."

The Summit Hills coach approached the microphone and began announcing his team to the crowd as Isaac hurried off. He finally caught sight of Mrs. Canavan in the far corner, away from the bleachers, almost hidden. Kevin was leaning against her. At first Isaac thought he was hugging his mother. But as he drew closer he could see that Kevin's hands were covering his ears.

"It's a lot for him," Mrs. Canavan said, answering before Isaac could ask what was wrong. "The loud music, the announcer, all the cheering."

The Summit Hills coach called out the names of two more players. They ran onto the court holding their hands high, and everyone continued clapping.

"I can tell Coach Park we don't want to be introduced," Isaac suggested. "Maybe Kevin and I could just sit on the bench."

Kevin turned toward Isaac when he heard his voice. When Isaac saw the frightened and confused look on his face, he remembered how Kevin had stood in the doorway alone for so many weeks, so shy and distant. How even when he'd worked up the courage to join his teammates at practice, he'd taken shot after shot in almost complete silence.

Sometimes Isaac forgot how far Kevin had come. But now, seeing Kevin so overwhelmed by the pounding music, the cheering crowds, and the brightly colored posters, Isaac remembered. Kevin was Kevin. Being part of a team wasn't easy for him. It would take every ounce of his courage to play today.

"You don't have to play if you don't want to," Isaac said. "We'll just watch."

Kevin nodded warily. Mrs. Canavan nodded too.

Isaac ran back to the Landmark bench. "Kevin and I don't want to be introduced and run out onto the floor," he explained to Coach Park, who was moving toward the microphone. "The noise, the crowd, it's all too much for him."

"No problem," Coach Park replied. "We can be flexible."

Maya had a suggestion. "Maybe we could introduce you guys and you could just wave from the corner."

"I guess we could try that," Isaac said.

So at the end of the team introductions,

Coach Park announced, "We have one more pair of Landmark players." He pointed to the far corner. "Isaac Burnett and Kevin Canavan." Isaac waved and nudged Kevin, who managed a small wave.

Coach Park continued. "Now please all rise and recite the Special Olympics oath."

Parents, friends, athletes, and partners all stood and said in one voice: "Let me win. But if I cannot win, let me be brave in the attempt."

The referees blew their whistles and the game began.

Theo and Phoenix scored baskets and pumped their fists in the air. The game stopped so that Shontelle and a Dolphin in a wheelchair could score baskets with Maya and Theo holding the barrel.

Isaac stayed with Kevin and his mother. He cheered every Landmark and Summit Hills basket. After Lucas tossed in a long basket, Isaac asked Kevin if he wanted to play.

Kevin leaned into his mother again and didn't respond.

"Come on," Isaac said, trying again. "I thought you were a shooter."

After a few seconds Kevin turned away from his mother, just as he had turned away from the doorway so many weeks ago. He walked slowly—as if he was testing each step—past the cheerleaders and shouting fans. Isaac, not sure where Kevin was going, stayed close behind. Finally Kevin took a seat at the end of the Landmark bench. He pulled his knees up to his chin, rocked gently back and forth, and watched the game. Isaac sat next to him and patted him on the back.

During a time out, Coach Park gathered the team around him. "Let's change things up a bit," he said. He looked past the huddle toward Kevin and Isaac. In a louder voice, he said, "Why don't we play Maya, Theo, Isaac, Kevin, Avi, and Lucas? And let's remember to pass the ball."

The moment Kevin heard his name, he stood up. Maya and Isaac traded nervous but hopeful glances. Isaac walked toward the other players and felt Kevin close beside

118

him, picking up his step. He was ready to play.

Summit Hills had the ball. Kevin raced so far back on defense that he almost ran off the court.

"Hands up!" Maya called out. Everyone—Kevin too—raised their hands high.

A Dolphins shot bounced off the rim. Isaac grabbed the rebound. He thought about getting Kevin the ball, but then he saw the disappointed look on the Dolphins player's face. Isaac handed her the ball and she happily shot again—and made it!

The whole crowd cheered.

Lucas dribbled slowly downcourt. He passed the ball to Kevin, who threw a too-long shot at the basket. The ball angled off the rim and bounced toward the far corner and into the crowd. Isaac raced after it. Mrs. Canavan tossed the ball into Isaac's hands and back into play.

Isaac turned and looked for Kevin. He was closer to the basket now. Isaac bounced him the ball. This time, Kevin's shot found the bottom of the bucket.

Swish!

Isaac jumped straight into the air. "All right!" he screamed. "Kevin, you *are* a shooter!"

Isaac raced upcourt. He felt like he had gotten the eighteenth out in a perfect game.

Isaac put a paper cup underneath the spout on the water jug and filled it up. He had just finished throwing twenty pitches in front of Coach Dorsett and Mr. Murakami, the pitching coach. The field was full of kids trying out for the T-bolts.

"You're looking good," his father said, standing near the jug. "Remember not to open up your shoulder, though. A couple of your fastballs were a little high in the zone."

Isaac didn't want to hear his dad's pitching instructions right now. He was more worried about his competition. "How do the other pitchers look?" he asked.

His father lowered his voice. "They look good, too—real good," he said. "They all throw pretty hard."

"Harder than me?"

"Some do, some don't. I'd put you somewhere in the middle."

Isaac finished the water in his cup.

His father dropped his voice to an even lower whisper. "It's gonna be close," he said. "It won't be easy to make this team."

Isaac knew that. "I'll just do my best."

"Okay, let's have everybody over here!" Coach Dorsett shouted, circling his hands above his head. "I want the pitchers to pitch in some real game situations, so the rest of you will bat and play the field. I'll call the game from in back of the pitcher's mound. C'mon. I need a catcher. Let's go."

When it was Isaac's turn to pitch, the coach put a runner on second and only two outfielders in the outfield. *Runner on second, nobody out*, he thought. *This coach is definitely not making it easy.*

Isaac gave himself a quick pep talk. *Do your best. You don't have to be perfect. Just take it one batter at a time. One pitch at a time.*

"Batter up!" Coach Dorsett shouted.

Isaac started the first batter with a changeup, down and away. The ball felt good as it left his hand.

"Ball one!" Coach Dorsett called.

Isaac wanted to argue the call, but he held back. *It's okay*, he told himself. *It's okay.*

Isaac's fastball slithered just an inch off the inside corner.

"Ball two."

Man, he's making it really tough, Isaac thought. But then he thought about the kids on the Sunday basketball team. *They don't give up. Just make this pitch a good one.*

Isaac fired a fastball at the outside corner. *Crack!* The ball bounced out to the shortstop, who checked the runner holding at second, then threw to first.

"One out, runner still on second," Coach Dorsett told the infielders.

Isaac kept his fastballs and changeups

low to the next batter. He worked the count full—three balls, two strikes. The batter slapped a grounder to second base. The runner took off as the second baseman fired the ball to first base just in time.

"Two outs, runner on third."

Isaac fell behind in the count to the next batter—two balls, one strike. He threw a darting changeup that the batter could only tap back to the mound. Isaac lobbed it to first base.

"Good job! Three outs, no runs," Coach Dorsett said. "All right, this inning let's start with a runner at third, no outs. Let's get a batter up there. C'mon, let's go."

Don't worry about the runner. Get the batter, Isaac told himself. The first batter lifted a fly ball far enough into left field that the runner at third tagged up and dashed home with a run.

"One out, one run."

Isaac tried to stay calm. *That's okay,* he reminded himself.

He got the next two batters out, one with a grounder to the shortstop and the other with a fly ball to shallow left field. He felt good as Coach Dorsett waved another pitcher onto the mound. *One run in two innings. No strikeouts, but I didn't give up any walks.*

"Great job," Isaac's dad said as Isaac gulped some cold water and wiped sweat from his forehead with the back of his other hand. "You weren't perfect, but—"

Isaac cut his father off. "Dad. I did the best I could in a tough situation. That's perfect enough." He realized he was starting to sound like Maya and almost smiled. Then he added: "I mean I'm happy with my performance."

His father smiled. "I guess you're right," he said. "I know I get carried away sometimes. Hey, I'd take you for *my* team anytime." Suddenly his phone starting ringing. His dad checked the number, then said, "I've got to take this, but grab your stuff and I'll meet you at the car."

As Isaac was gathering his things, Mr. Murakami approached him. "Nice job today," the pitching coach said, looking down at his clipboard. "You threw strikes. You spotted your fastball and mixed in a good changeup. You took it one batter—one pitch—at a time." He paused for a moment, as if he was trying to remember something. "You're Isaac Burnett, right?"

"Yes sir," Isaac said a little too loudly.

"You had a real good season this year with the Giants, didn't you?"

"I was 6–0." Then Isaac quickly added, "The team did well too. We were 11–4."

"Michael Park's your coach, right?"

"Yes sir."

Coach Murakami checked his notes again. "The summer league is pretty tough. But you look like someone who can handle it."

"Yes sir."

"I just talked to Coach Dorsett," Coach Murakami said with a smile and a nod. "We're picking our pitchers today. We're going to need a deep bullpen and we think you've got what it takes to be a Thunderbolt."

Isaac's heart almost jumped out of his

chest. He could hardly believe what he was hearing. He'd made it! He was going to play for the Thunderbolts!

"Thank you, sir! That's awesome!"

He couldn't wait to tell his dad, his mom, Coach Park—and Kevin.

Chapter 16

The Landmark school gym was so empty that the sound of Isaac's sneakers squeaking across the floor echoed against the walls.

Maya was helping her father pull basketballs out of his big brown equipment bag.

"Hey, Coach," Isaac called. "Hi, Maya."

Coach Park smiled. "You're early. Good. Will you and Maya get our barrel from the back for Shontelle and put it against the wall? I want her to score plenty of baskets today."

"I made the Thunderbolts!" The news seemed to burst out of Isaac.

Maya's eyes lit up. "Isaac! You rock!"

"Fantastic!" Coach Park agreed. "I'm not

surprised. The T-bolts are getting a really good pitcher. You'll give them a chance to win."

Isaac grinned. "Thanks, Coach. I guess 6–0 isn't too bad."

Coach Park pulled the last ball from the bag. "I think you got even better as the season went along," he said. "You learned a lot."

"Yeah," Isaac agreed. "One thing I learned was that I didn't have to be perfect every game, every pitch. I've gotten better at not giving up."

Isaac looked around the Landmark gym and thought about that Sunday weeks ago when he rushed down the stairs for his first practice.

"I told you that you'd learn something coming here," Coach said. "Remember?"

"I remember. You were right." Isaac smiled. "So how many more Sunday practices do we have?"

"Just this one," Coach Park said, tossing him a basketball. "Then we switch sports in a couple of weeks."

"To what?"

"Bowling."

"Bowling?"

"Yeah. Do you bowl?" Maya asked.

"Not really," Isaac said. "But I could help out."

"You'll be pretty busy this summer with the T-bolts," Coach Park warned him.

"No worries. I'll find the time."

Just then Phoenix, Lucas, and Theo rushed into the gym along with their parents, breaking up the quiet of the space.

"Where's the ball?" Phoenix demanded. "I want to take some shots!" Isaac bounced him a pass and the lefty flipped a quick jumper at the basket. Theo began to sing and Lucas gave Coach Park a big hug.

A minute later Kevin raced in, grabbed a basketball, and started shooting. Isaac could only stare. Maya came up behind him and whispered, "A little different from that first time, huh?"

"Yeah, real different," he said as one of Kevin's shots ricocheted off the rim right toward Isaac. "I'd better get busy," he said as he caught the ball on a bounce and headed toward his teammate. "Hey, Kevin, you need a rebounder?"

Kevin pointed at Isaac with both hands. "You're a rebounder," he said. "I'm a shooter."

Isaac flipped him a pass and Kevin tossed up his two-handed shot.

Swish!

Before Isaac could get his hands on the ball, Kevin called, "Courtesy!"

Isaac smiled and got him the ball.

Kevin's next shot rattled around the rim and fell off. Isaac grabbed the rebound and dribbled to the corner. "Hey, I made the Thunderbolts," he said and let go a long jump shot.

Kevin grabbed the ball. "Thunderbolts?" he asked, squinting at Isaac.

"It's another baseball team," Isaac explained. "It's sort of a summer all-star team. I'm going to pitch for them."

"Go, Giants! Go, Thunderbolts!" Kevin shouted.

Isaac rebounded Kevin's shot and bounced

him a pass. "Hey, are you going to do the bowling team with Coach Park?"

Kevin made a motion as if he were rolling a ball toward a set of ten pins. "I'm a bowler," he declared.

Isaac laughed. "Then so am I," he said. "Then so am I."

Perfect Games

Coach Park knows his baseball. A perfect game—that is when a pitcher pitches a whole game and doesn't allow a single batter to get on base—doesn't happen very often. And sometimes a perfect game depends more on luck than skill.

Isaac needed 18 straight outs for his perfect game because the games in his league were six innings long. Games in Major League Baseball are nine innings, so a pro pitcher has to get 27 straight outs for a perfect game.

As of fall 2012, there have only been 23 perfect games in Major League Baseball—

and MLB began in the 1870s! While some of those games were thrown by Hall of Fame pitchers such as Cy Young, Sandy Koufax, and Jim "Catfish" Hunter, many others were thrown by pitchers whose overall records were not so impressive. Here is a list of those pitchers, along with the year they pitched their perfect game and their career win-loss record (as of fall 2012).

Philip Humber	2012	16–15
Dallas Braden	2010	26–36
Mike Witt	1984	117–116
Len Barker	1981	74–76
Don Larsen	1956	81–91
Charlie Robertson	1922	49–80
Lee Richmond	1880	75–100

Richmond pitched the first perfect game in baseball history, for the Worcester (Massachusetts) Ruby Legs against the Cleveland Blues. (The Ruby Legs dropped out of the National League after the 1882 season.)

Amazingly, Robertson pitched his perfect game in one of his first major league starts.

But he never had a winning season during his eight-year career.

Don Larsen pitched baseball's most famous perfect game. The game is so well known because Larsen got 27 straight outs for the New York Yankees in the crucial fifth game of the 1956 World Series against the Brooklyn Dodgers (they later became the Los Angeles Dodgers). The Yankees went on to win the Series that year in seven games.

Larsen was no superstar. Although he had an 11–5 record and a 3.26 earned run average in 1956, just two years earlier he had been the biggest loser in baseball, posting a 3–21 record with the Baltimore Orioles. But Larsen was perfect on that October 8, 1956, afternoon in Yankee Stadium.

The list of 23 perfect games does not include three games that, except for a bit of bad luck, would have been perfect.

Harvey Haddix in 1959 and Pedro Martinez in 1995 pitched games in which they retired 27 straight batters. But in each of those games the score was tied 0–0 after nine innings, sending them into extra innings. Each pitcher gave up a hit in the later innings, so their efforts are not counted as perfect games. Incredibly, Haddix had pitched 12 perfect innings—*36 straight outs*—only to lose the game (and his perfect game) in the 13th inning, 1–0.

In 2010, Armando Galarraga of the Detroit Tigers set down 26 straight Cleveland Indian batters. He needed only one more out for a perfect game. The 27th batter bounced a grounder to the Tigers first baseman. Galarraga raced over to cover the bag, caught the toss from the first baseman, and tagged first base for what appeared to be the last out. But the umpire, Jim Joyce, called the runner safe. Galarraga's chance at a perfect game—and a place in baseball history— was gone. But Galarraga didn't get upset. He got the next Cleveland batter and the win.

Film later showed that Joyce had made the wrong call—the Cleveland runner was clearly out. After the game, Joyce apologized for his mistake. The next day, the Tigers were playing and Joyce was behind home plate again. Usually a team's manager presents the lineup card to the umpire before the game. But on that day, in a great show of sportsmanship, Galarraga presented the lineup card to Joyce and shook his hand. "Nobody's perfect," Galarraga said.

Galarraga had missed his perfect game. But he had been a good sport. Galarraga knew, just as Isaac learned in this book, that in sports, sometimes there are more important things than being perfect.

Special Olympics

Special Olympics Unified Sports teams play many different sports all over the world. The Unified Sports program was started in the 1980s when Eunice Kennedy Shriver, the founder of Special Olympics, and others in the Special Olympics movement noticed that the athletes with intellectual disabilities played with just each other.

The Special Olympics organizers decided to start a program with their athletes playing together with non-disabled partners as teammates. Their aim was to give their athletes an interesting opportunity to improve their skills, have fun, and make new friends.

Now, more than 220,000 athletes with intellectual disabilities play Special Olympics Unified Sports with more than 320,000 partners. Even more athletes and partners will play in the future when Special Olympics expands its Unified Sports program.

Some Special Olympics athletes play at a competitive level. I saw a soccer game at Catholic University in Washington, D.C., in which athletes with intellectual disabilities played on the same teams and on equal terms with students from Madeira School, a private high school in McLean, Virginia. When I asked the Madeira kids what surprised them about the Special Olympics athletes, one student smiled and said, "Some of them are *really* good."

Other Special Olympics Unified Sports teams are more like Mr. Park's recreational basketball team. The partners, like Isaac and Maya, make an effort not to dominate play. Instead, they give the Special Olympics athletes like Kevin, Theo, and Shontelle a chance to improve their skills.

Special Olympics Unified Sports was started for the benefit of athletes with intellectual disabilities. But the Unified Sports partners without disabilities have found that they get a lot out of the practices and games too. Like Isaac, the partners learn about not giving up and trying their best even when things are not going their way. The important thing is that on all Special Olympics Unified Sports teams the athletes and partners are teammates. And sometimes, just like on any team, the teammates become friends.

To find out more about Special Olympics Unified Sports, visit the Special Olympics website: www.specialolympics.org.

Note: The Spread the Word to End the Word campaign, created in 2009 by two college students, continues to make great strides in its fight to eliminate the use of the word *retarded* or *retard* when referring to people with intellectual disabilities or when referring to any person doing something foolish.

To find out more, go to www.r-word.org.

Acknowledgments

Lots of people helped with this book. Tim Shriver, chairman and CEO of Special Olympics, took time out of his busy schedule to meet with me for breakfast and share his experience and expertise. He is carrying on the great work of his mother, Eunice Kennedy Shriver, the founder of Special Olympics.

Kirsten Seckler and Mandy Murphy at Special Olympics reviewed parts of the manuscript dealing with Special Olympics Unified Sports. Their comments made the book better.

Robert "Beau" Doherty, President of Special Olympics Connecticut, gave me many valuable details about the history of the Special Olympics Unified Sports movement. That is, when we weren't talking about the Boston Red Sox.

I am also indebted to Jayne Dixon Weber of the National Fragile X Foundation, who reviewed portions of the book to help make sure I presented Kevin in a realistic way. More information about fragile X syndrome can be found on the Foundation's website at www.fragilex.org.

I spent several weekends watching the Special Olympics Unified Sports basketball team at Blessed Sacrament School in Washington, D.C. Dave Ficca is the team's coach. Dave and his wife Meredith were generous enough to share their stories about being the parents of two Special Olympics athletes, D. J. and Matt.

Pamela Yerg, the area director of Special Olympics Montgomery County (SOMO) in Maryland, helped by putting me in touch with the Ficcas and the Unified Sports team at Blessed Sacrament.

The information about the Special Olympics Unified Sports program came from my interviews with Tim Shriver, Beau Doherty, Pam Yerg, and the Ficcas. I also consulted several documents concerning Special Olympics Unified Sports provided by Special Olympics.

The information about the perfect games in Major League Baseball came from several sources, including *The Baseball Encyclopedia* (4th edition); the wonderful baseball website www.baseball-reference.com; as well as *Sports Illustrated* magazine and the *Washington Post*.

And thanks go to my son Liam Bowen, pitching coach and recruiting coordinator at University of Maryland Baltimore County (UMBC). He reviewed the pitching portions of this book.

Last but certainly not least, I want to thank my wife Peggy Jackson. As with each of my books, she helped me every step of the way. For that and much more, I am grateful.

About the Author

Fred Bowen was a Little Leaguer who loved to read. Now he is the author of many action-packed books of sports fiction. He has also written a weekly sports column for kids in the *Washington Post* since 2000.

Bowen played lots of sports growing up. For thirteen years, he coached kids' baseball, soccer, and basketball teams. Some of his stories spring directly from his coaching experience and his sports-happy childhood in Marblehead, Massachusetts.

Bowen was a lawyer for many years before retiring to become a full-time children's author. He has been a guest author at schools and conferences across the country, as well as the Smithsonian Institute in Washington, DC, and The Baseball Hall of Fame.

He now lives in Silver Spring, Maryland, with his wife Peggy Jackson. They have two grown children.

www.fredbowen.com

HEY, SPORTS FANS!

Don't miss these action-packed books by Fred Bowen...

Real Hoops
PB: $5.95 / 978-1-56145-566-9 / 1-56145-566-0
Hud can run, pass, and shoot at top speed. But he's not much of a team player. Can Ben convince Hud to leave his dazzling—but one-man—style back on the asphalt?

Quarterback Season
PB: $5.95 / 978-1-56145-594-2 / 1-56145-594-6
Matt expects to be the starting quarterback. But after a few practices watching Devro, a talented seventh grader, he's starting to get nervous. To make matters worse, his English teacher is on his case about a new class assignment: a journal.

Go for the Goal!
PB: $5.95 / 978-1-56145-632-1 / 1-56145-632-2
Josh and his talented travel league soccer teammates are having trouble coming together as a successful team—until he convinces them to try team-building exercises.

Perfect Game
PB: $5.95 / 978-1-56145-594-2 / 1-56145-594-6
Isaac is determined to pitch a perfect game—no hits, no runs, no walks, and no errors. He gets close a couple of times, but when things go wrong he can't get his head back in the game. Then Isaac meets an interesting Unified Sports basketball player who shows him a whole new way to think about *perfect*.

Check out **www.SportsStorySeries.com** for more info.

All-St★r Sports Story
Series

T. J.'s Secret Pitch
PB: $5.95 / 978-1-56145-504-1 / 1-56145-504-0

T. J.'s pitches just don't pack the power they need to strike out
the batters, but the story of 1940s baseball hero Rip Sewell
and his legendary eephus pitch may help him find a solution.

The Golden Glove
PB: $5.95 / 978-1-56145-505-8 / 1-56145-505-9

Without his lucky glove, Jamie doesn't believe in his ability to
lead his baseball team to victory. How will he learn that faith
in oneself is the most important equipment for any game?

The Kid Coach
PB: $5.95 / 978-1-56145-506-5 / 1-56145-506-7

Scott and his teammates can't find an adult to coach their
team, so they must find a leader among themselves.

Playoff Dreams
PB: $5.95 / 978-1-56145-507-2 / 1-56145-507-5

Brendan is one of the best players in the league, but no
matter how hard he tries, he can't make his team win.

Winners Take All
PB: $5.95 / 978-1-56145-512-6 / 1-56145-512-1

Kyle makes a poor decision to cheat in a big game.
Someone discovers the truth and threatens to reveal it.
What can Kyle do now?

All-St★r Sports Story
Series

Full Court Fever
PB: $5.95 / 978-1-56145-508-9 / 1-56145-508-3

The Falcons have the skill but not the height to win their games. Will the full-court zone press be the solution to their problem?

Off the Rim
PB: $5.95 / 978-1-56145-509-6 / 1-56145-509-1

Hoping to be more than a benchwarmer, Chris learns that defense is just as important as offense.

The Final Cut
PB: $5.95 / 978-1-56145-510-2 / 1-56145-510-5

Four friends realize that they may not all make the team and that the tryouts are a test—not only of their athletic skills, but also of their friendship.

On the Line
PB: $5.95 / 978-1-56145-511-9 / 1-56145-511-3

Marcus is the highest scorer and the best rebounder, but he's not so great at free throws—until the school custodian helps him overcome his fear of failure.

Check out **www.SportsStorySeries.com** for more info.